Ms *Guided* ANGELS

notionpress.com

INDIA · SINGAPORE · MALAYSIA

Ms *Guided* ANGELS

Second Edition

A business at risk. Many lives at stake.
A friendship tested.

SANGEETA MALHOTRA
SHRUTI SAXENA

notionpress.com

INDIA • SINGAPORE • MALAYSIA

Second Edition 2025

ISBN 978-93-84878-20-7

AUTHOR'S NOTE

We believe that we all have a force that guides us through our lives. It tells us what is right for us, who are in the wrong; it lets us know when we have sinned and when we deserve a "feel good" day for a deed well done. We call it our conscience, our intuition, a sixth sense. But what is it really?

We have pondered on this question and have come to embrace a childish, innocent belief. The belief that we all have our own customized angels that we elect before we embark on this tenuous journey we call "life". We hold them in esteem and, therefore, entrust them with this most prestigious role, of guarding us so that we may falter and fall but not so as to plummet into an abyss, never to return.

It is a tough job but these spiritual beings must try to protect us; protect us from bodily harm, from evil influences, and mostly from ourselves.

But the most difficult part of the role is that they must help us even when we feel we don't need it and never realize that it exists.

There are, however, a few of us who are truly lucky. And these are the ones whose paths get entwined. These are the ones who are touched by their angel.

Being human, they may fight and argue, agree to constantly disagree, love to hate each other. But in all this mayhem, they change each other, forever.

This is what happened to two young, independent women finding their footing in today's corporate space. This book is set in the *"Right now and here to stay"* booming industry of Business Process Outsourcing. And that is where Faith and Naina begin their search for their true destinies, and peace, together.

In this story, we will take you through Faith's mysterious existence. In contrast, Naina will seem unconvincingly simple and the typical, little *Miss Goody Two Shoes.*

While humor'll be lost on Faith, Naina will laugh with ease. While Faith will peak your curiosity, Naina will steal your hearts. And while Faith will live life on the edge and pick at her wounds, Naina will avoid confrontations and complicate matters more still. You'll never find two people more different but, together, they will create magic and you shall be a witness.

This is not just "a" story but also OUR story. We have brought out Faith and Naina from our souls and they are real.

Although dramatized, to relay the significance of certain events on our being and, maybe more so, to keep our loved ones' private lives hidden, this book hopes to unravel the depth of our friendship in light of extenuating circumstances.

The tales of hypocrisy, politicking, jealousy, and sacrilege, detailed in this book may have indeed happened… all in the name of professional advancement. However, these are neither drawn from any particular organization nor represent deeds committed by anyone living or dead.

For those of us who have had the misfortune of having worked for a large multi-national or, even worse, an Indian company would question what the hue and cry is about. Professional misdemeanor is the oldest trick in the book.

But read on and discover a never before braved effort to capture the perils of a man's world through the eyes of a woman. For, even though, there's no doubt that today's woman can outdo a man in 'most every aspect of life, at work, she still remains a victim of slander, sexual innuendos and worse.

So come and be a part of our lives, as we see 'em … cherish 'em… live 'em.

Shruti & Sangeeta

Petals of Love, that soulful laughter,
The voice of God,
Who said that life ain't odd?
For it's true, my dear friend,
That you are here, and I am here,
God's lovely creations,
And all that is Holy.
But, in all our joy and rejoice...
And this is odd,
That, 'round the corner, lives an evil man.
"Crimson tides, cold mountains, cruel deserts is what life is", he says,
"Vanity, faithlessness and folly".
"No!" we cry,
"Truth is our being, Trust is our heart.
This is the circle of life, old man".
"We hold on..."

"This book is for our kids Aanya (Shruti's daughter)
and Saamy (Sangeeta's canine son),
who are our world !"

CONTENTS

PROLOGUE

FINDING THE WITNESS

Faith Jones closed her eyes in thoughtful silence. She always found the twilight hours relaxing and perfect for practicing her newfound love: Meditation.

Today, however, Faith was restless and slightly annoyed at her lack of concentration. Her mind kept drifting off to her infuriating colleagues at work, her hair styling appointment the day after, her dog that would need to be walked soon, her past, her life... everything except for the task at hand. "Focus, Faith! You can do this", she muttered and readied herself once again.

Modern physiology, scientific research, says that between the two eyebrows is the gland, which is the most mysterious part in the body. This gland, called the pineal gland, is the third eye of the Tibetans – *Shivanetra:* the eye of Shiva, of tantra. Between the two eyes there is a third eye existing but ordinarily it is non-functioning. You have to do something about it to open it. It is not blind. It is simply closed. When you attain complete focus at the third eye, suddenly you become a witness. Through the third eye, you can see thoughts running like clouds in the sky or people moving on the street. You become an observer and, sometimes, you become the very essence of breath, *prana.* In this, you become clairvoyant!

Faith had become enchanted with this technique when she had heard of it. After having practiced it for months, she had attained some measure of success and had become more content and at peace, as an individual. "Attention between the eyebrows, let the mind be before thought" Faith pressed on. Her breathing became deeper and her body felt lighter.

Faith realized that she had a lot going for her. She hailed from a well-known family in the metropolis. She was an extremely attractive brunette, tall with a fabulous figure to match, 28 and very attached. She was also very aware of the fact that she, Faith Jones, was a catch!

"Become a witness... simply observe all thoughts that enter your mind. Keep the focus..." Faith's eyelids fluttered. Her mind was now completely coordinated with her breathing. "Breathe in... Follow the path that the fresh oxygen takes through your body... Slowly, breathe out".

For the first time, Faith began to see vibrant images through her mind's eye. "Such bright colors!" she thought. They were so vivid that she physically felt her eyes smart. Faith knew that she was coming to experience a strange phenomenon.

Suddenly, she saw images that realized her worst nightmare and she was shocked! She gasped for air and jumped out of her stance, violently! Although, she was now out of her meditative state, she realized that she was shivering and had broken out in a cold sweat. "That was completely surreal!" Faith said abashed.

Faith justified this as just another experience towards cleansing her mind off the recent events in her life. Her joining a leading Business Process Outsourcing company, Stan Inc., as a Quality Manager had opened her eyes to corporate political dominion in a new *vistar*. The BPO industry has it's own dynamics as did Stan Inc. The industry is fairly young of just about 10 years. The people who joined this industry as young college graduates are now 30 odd year olds and leading large divisions at extremely high positions, and even higher salaries. Needless to say, this kind of power, and resources, goes to their heads and modesty becomes a rare find. The workplace becomes their playground and politicking their forte.

Faith also, however, saw the benefits that this industry had bestowed on the Indian economy, the growing purchasing power, the exponentially growing employment opportunities, the excellent work ethics, for the most part. She had, in such a short time, developed an unbridled passion for this company and the young people who worked for her processes. They had so much energy and commitment for those just out of college and starting their careers.

She had also found love. Much to her complete surprise and amazement, she had found love in their dynamic, gorgeous hunk of a client. He had whisked her off her feet on their first meeting and it had been a roller coaster ride ever since. Edwin, of part Indian-part Mexican origin; Edwin, of late night calls and beautiful dreams; Edwin, of sweetness and brilliance; Edwin, who could do no wrong!

She dragged herself to the kitchen, opened the refrigerator door and picked out her favorite mineral water bottle. She gulped down half the contents in one draw and balanced her delicate frame on the counter. She was now feeling a little more human and she let down a sigh of relief convincing her that this was just her mind playing games. She, then, trampled to the adjoining dining room and decided she would watch a spot of television.

Faith realized that she had an addiction. To her, watching television, incessantly, was a necessary modern evil. She flicked the channels and landed on the news. "How boring! Nothing but murder, molestation, theft, corruption. Blah!"

Faith raised her arm to move on to her favorite channel when she stopped short. Her eyes fell on her mobile and she saw a blinker for an unread message from her supervisor, Surinder Singh. As she read it, her mouth fell open with shock, her throat constricted with fear, and a chill ran up her spine.

Faith felt her anger rising giving way to helplessness as she looked on.

The message read, "All Hands on Deck. Edwin is stopping the current ramp-up of 100 underwriters"

Her worst nightmare had, indeed, come true!

Her life had again come full circle. With promises of more business, that Edwin had never intended to keep, he had put at risk the careers of the 100 people hired for the business? How would Faith save grace? And how could Faith let another man betray her again?

PART ONE

THE ORIGINS

Delhi and NCR
3 months before the incident

Chapter 1
INHERITANCE

Wearing a black, custom fit, satin finish, chanel suit and her customary frown, Faith pushed through the crowd of local, weekend shoppers. She had no patience for the loud, demanding women shoppers scathing the poor shopkeepers with their fire tongues and bargaining to the last paisa. It offended her when anyone treated others with scorn and disrespect. Faith was a true believer in equality across gender, race, religion and position in society.

Treading a little faster now, Faith re-adjusted her grip on her patent leather Gucci handbag and turned her complete concentration on saving her precious Minolo stilettos from the gooey muck on the roadside. Finally, she reached her destination.

It was a decrepit, old building just off the main market that once had a beautiful mural of pretty girls, in exquisite dancing postures, on the façade. Now, it was just a display of horrific vulgarity, pornographic suggestiveness and vile obscenities.

"Typical disregard for property!" Faith leaned against the wall and closed her eyes for a moment's rest. She was tired. She was emotionally distraught and slightly apprehensive about her joining a new organization the following day. Why had she chosen this role when she had no real need to get into a Business Process Outsourcing company? She had excellent credentials and education and she could continue in the financial institution that she was working in earlier. Anyhow, she had been offered a good deal and she knew she could ace this one! Nevertheless, her heart tugged at her. She knew her heart was beating faster than normal and it wasn't just the walk from the parking lot to this building nor was it the meeting she was here for… or was it?

She had been uncomfortable with the idea when one of her cousins had suggested it to her. But things had reached a stage where she needed help. She would not make it alone. She needed to know why these things kept happening to her… she needed answers! Before she had a change of heart, she hurried inside the main door. She still could not believe that life had brought her here. She was a bright, intelligent, healthy, young woman…well, maybe not healthy enough. She was about to see a shrink!

Faith, unlike other kids hailing from ultra-rich families, had not had an easy childhood... far from it. She had lived as an orphan since she was 17 but, then, she had always been more mature for her age. She had developed early and, even then, had a figure most maidens would die for. Her rich mahogany complexion and long hair, lustrous and black, only added to her charm and she learnt survival techniques the hard way… by warding off advances from teenage boys that wanted to "*play*".

Although she came from money, Faith never really let it go to her head. She had remained rooted in that sense. She, however, presented herself with a lot of attitude. She spoke with an English accent. In her behavior she was not heated, but cool. She offered a very aloof, distant, groomed, in-ward, irreligious persona to people.

Life is about discovering yourself and others. Faith felt that she had always gotten hurt when she got close to discovering herself *with* others. So, she had stopped. She did not care to dwell on her past, never spoke about her childhood, and told people she did not remember her parents or that fateful accident. The truth, however, was still the truth.

Faith. She hated her name. She had stopped relating to it. That had been a long time ago, in another lifetime.

Chapter 2
IN-DEPTH

The strokes of the brush went back and forth on the stretched canvas with wild, careless abandon, leaving behind rich streaks of her favorite colors. The effect was startling, thought provoking, devastatingly beautiful; an abstract work of art, vibrant, yet raw and untamed. It reminded her of her own persona, simple yet striking. Naina looked at her creation and smiled. Yes! She liked it.

Content, she slowly backed away from her work.

She was extremely attached to each of her paintings. She had started working on this one around a week back with no clear thought in mind as to what she wanted to depict. However, for the past two days, she had had this sudden urge to finish it. This passion had taken over her completely and she had forgotten everything else but her tools and her canvas.

"Joe!" she shrieked excitedly. "Come, see this!"

As she waited eagerly for her studio assistant to come in, she caught her reflection in the glass door of her studio. And, then, she laughed. It was a melodious, throaty laughter. People had often told her that it was sincere and highly infectious.

Her white shirt was no longer white, with various hues of reds, yellows and orange splashed on. Her ruddy pants were far from their original black. She had paint on her hands, face and hair... almost everywhere that it could possible go. With her unkempt hair, oversized clothes and bare feet, she looked like a masterpiece herself!

Joe caught her still giggling at her appearance when he entered. To him, no one had ever looked more beautiful. Blessed with exquisite milk 'n peaches complexion and the most intense almond eyes that shone with each of her warm, radiant smiles, Naina could melt any heart. Naina Chopra was an attractive woman!

Joe continued to study her, as she was busy packing her paints, brushes and other accessories. She sensed his presence in the room and turned.

Still, he remained rooted.

It was times like these that embarrassed him. In spite of himself, he could not turn his gaze away. He was mesmerized.

"What're you staring at, silly? What took you so long?", Naina said smiling. "I can't wait to show you. I'm done!" Naina's face was beaming.

Naina held Joe's arm and almost dragged him across the room to the canvas. She liked Joe and valued his opinion, of her works, tremendously.

Naina had turned the canvas's front to face the wall. She always liked to dramatize such important moments. She picked up the painting delicately but before revealing it to Joe, she pleaded, "You must tell me your first thought on seeing it. Promise?"

Joe crossed his heart and then his arms, waiting expectantly for the grand curtain raiser!

"Voila!" In one slick move, Naina flipped it around to face Joe.

It was breathtaking! "It's a visual treat, Naina! I think... No! I know that you have outdone yourself this time, Babe! I can almost feel the richness. I sooo want to touch it right now." squealed Joe as took a greedy step forward toward the precious creation.

"Don't you dare! The touching'll have to wait till it dries out. But you really mean what you just said?" Naina was smiling, ear-to-ear. This had to be her best day ever!

"This is a jackpot, honey! It don't get better than this. No more painting in ol' broken down hatches anymore. It'll be the red carpet, I tell ya."

Naina mounted the frame on the easel and looked at it adoringly. "It feel its so me yet there's a huge part that I have yet to discover... I get this tingling every time I look at it. I have a strange feeling... almost as if it's telling me something."

"What does it say?" Joe was intrigued. He propped himself on a stool and rested his face on the small of his palm. He always liked an artist's story for a painting, especially Naina's. This time, he was certain that it would be deep. He had never seen Naina's eyes shine with such fervor.

"Look at this area. It's right there... yet it's not the focal point. I didn't even notice it till I studied it just now but it's my favorite part of the picture" explained Naina.

"Now that you mention it... I was wondering what was pulling me to the painting. And this is it! So simple yet completely intriguing."

Naina continued, barely waiting for Joe to finish. Her eyes were running madly over her. She began to pace the floor of the small workshop as she carried on. "The rest of the painting is a collation of activity... rough impressions of visual thoughts in my head at the time. But this is so peaceful, which is weird because this is where everything else on the painting unite. The wild, bold strokes in basic colours collide with the more textured, deliberate splashes."

"It's when time stood still for me. I remember those moments when my mind stopped "thinking"! My hands were moving while my mind was still, at peace. Wonder, how did my hands know their job?"

Naina's voice had risen to a passionately tense note. She was so close to artistic release. So close to genius! She suddenly stopped, once more before the mirror. When she spoke again, her voice was calm. And she finished her analysis of her work with:

"To me, it's beautiful because I did not create this… it was created for me."

Naina sighed as she staring at her reflection, unseeing. When Joe caught her eyes, he smiled affectionately. He was so proud of her. She smiled back. She had tears in her eyes.

"What'll you call it", Joe asked softly.

Naina took a deep breath before answering. "It smells of the times to come, of new beginnings. I'll call it Originations".

✻✻✻

In her excitement at finishing her artwork, naina had forgotten all about work and it was late.

She grabbed her bag and hurried outside to catch an *Auto-Rickshaw*.

As she stepped into the madness of the central market, she scanned the jammed roads for a ride back home.

Across the road, she suddenly noticed an impeccably dressed woman, in all black, bent down on the pavement. Ordinarily, Naina would not have noticed. But, there was something instinctively wrong with this picture. It seemed like this woman was cleaning the bottom of her very impractical shoes.

'What are the likes of her doing in a place like this?' the artist in Naina questioned.

She moved a little further to the right to catch a glimpse of the face when the woman picked up something and all that Naina could see were her long, gorgeous curls flowing down her shoulders to cover the side of her face.

There was a distinct style about her that caught Naina's attention. But, instinctively, she gave Naina cold vibes, even from a distance. She couldn't see the woman's face, however her entire body language shouted, "Touch me not or else!"

'What could she be so interested in?' Naina wondered!

Just then, the lady in black turned and Naina saw a cute, little puppy, from the street, whimpering in her arms. It was clear from the blood flowing freely from one of its paws that it had been just hit by one of the vehicles on the road. The woman was trying to stop the bleeding.

This discovery surprised her, pleasantly. 'Perceptions! I must remember to not judge a book by its cover', Naina spoke aloud. She was crazy about dogs herself and admired this gesture. She started to move towards them, but before she could cross the road, the kind woman along with the puppy was gone.

❀❀❀

'Catch him yash! He's run away with my shoe. He'll eat it up!' Screamed naina.

Naina and Yash, her husband, were running, in circles, all over the house looking for their dog Randy and the shoe, in question.

She had just returned home, begun to change when the little terror had attacked.

'Randy, come here, at once! Give it back to Mommy, 'ordered Yash. It had no effect, whatsoever, on the dog who had sneaked under the bed and was happily chewing at the shoe.

The shoe had no hopes for survival.

Yash and Naina had met nearly six years ago at a music concert in Bangalore where he was performing. He is a ghazal singer, and a very popular one at that, with a huge fan following. She had been working at the time, as a "Collections" associate, in one of India's primary banks and had won the ticket to his concert in a special contest. She had exceeded her targets and come to Bangalore to redeem her prize.

And what a prize it was!

They had met at the after show reception dinner, and for Yash, it had been love at first strike. She on the other hand was too 'cool' about the whole thing, as she was not looking for a relationship.

She had given a go ahead to her parents to look for a suitable match for her and was mentally prepared to go in for an arranged set-up. However, Yash had had other plans! He had turned on all his charm on her and for days tried to woo her.

He was completely bowled over her carefree style and her 'I don't care a damn' attitude. He admired her sensibility and soft emotions.

For Naina, mental compatibility was most important and Yash fitted the bill perfectly. He was a good man and she needed that in her husband more than anything else. Finally, she melted.

After eight months of courtship, he had proposed marriage and she had said, "Yippee!"

That day had been a milestone in Naina's life.

It had been six years since then.

'I've come a long away', she thought, as she got ready to go to work.

Naina was a Senior Manager, heading the 'NIGO' (Not In Good Order) process for a Mortgage Client in the BPO (Business Process Outsourcing) division in Stan Inc.

Chapter 3
AN OLD FRIEND

A wise little lady had once proclaimed,

"I drink champagne when I'm happy and when I'm sad.

Sometimes I drink it when I'm alone. When I have company, I consider it obligatory.

I trifle with it if I'm not hungry and drink it when I am.

Otherwise I never touch it – unless I'm thirsty".

Faith smiled as she consoled herself with that thought. With a glass of her favorite Zinfandel, she went back to another timeless thriller by James Patterson, an author she admired ardently for his pulse pounding tales and harrowing plots.

The book at hand was set in the 11th century and spelled a breathtaking saga about a common man who stretched his means to the limit, and then some; to achieve his life's true purpose and serve God's own will, all this in the face of the greatest of sacrifices and sacrilege. This especially haunting portrayal of the horror and the ghastly torture that was inflicted upon the meek, by the unrelenting lords of the 11th Century, was no matter for a joker. "The Jester", however, was a book about one.

As she read on, Faith got more and more engrossed in the lilting pace of the book. She was an intense person, and got into the mood of what she read, and lived each character! No wonder that post a glass of wine, down, Faith was howling. She let the tears stream down her face without wiping them away. She liked to feel the pain, till it hurt really badly, till she could feel it travel down to her fingers and every part of her being. This was important to her. She would not have been alive without this. This was the only time she ***felt***.

"There are people in this world who make the things, I find special, the most grotesque and repugnant. These are the people I've cared about. I once was a simple person but I faced that which I wish not, for even my worst enemies: the destruction of my only dream, the dream of a sweet, innocent young girl. And, then, I forgot that I was a good human being", Faith thought wryly as she poured herself another drink.

✿✿✿

She was running as fast as her legs would carry her. She slowed her pace a tad bit only to catch her breath and sneak a peak at the tall, handsome man, steadily closing the gap between them.

She dashed around one of the mighty rocks on the beach and just escaped as a strong arm fell short of grasping her forearm. Her sudden turn befuddled her pursuer and, taking advantage of her position on the beach, she dashed into the cold water of the Indian Ocean.

The shock of that stride took her breath away and her lilting laughter got caught in her throat. She, however, dove side first till she was completed submerged and could swim away from the shore, under water.

As she came up for air, she was smiling. Her gorgeous man was standing on the beach; his hands on his waist with the most amused look on his face. The sight of him made her happy and she laughed her heartiest laughter before she began to mock him with her "different strokes".

She knew he was impressed and she had beaten him once again. She had once been a professional sprinter and swimmer, even if that was only when she was 15! She was still in excellent shape.

He challenged her, to come out of the water, with his eyes and his wicked-sweet smile. Her heart did a somersault whenever he gave her that look and she could do nothing except to bow down to all his wishes. It melted her to her soul.

She swam in to meet her man and, as he pulled her out into his arms, she knew that she loved him. Faith loved Rohan like, she thought, she could never love any man. He was the first man she had loved and would be the last. He was her husband and she was a one-man woman.

Just as she had this plethora of thoughts sweep over her like a warm blanket on a winter night, she felt a chill run through her. Her entire body convulsed with a sharp pain emanating from her torso. “Am I having a heart attack?” Faith thought.

She looked up into Rohan’s face and parted her lips to speak but no words came. Her legs were starting to give and she was feeling helpless. Her eyes swelled up with unsung tears as she searched Rohan’s eyes. They reminded her of a shark’s, hard and cold, unfeeling yet emoting.

And then she understood. She looked down at the source of her pain. Her heart. She could see it as plainly as the ocean. The knife was like his eyes, hard and cold.

Faith rocked herself back and forth, back and forth, and again. She was crying herself to bed again. She wondered when her nightmares would spare her and offer her a good night’s sleep.

The psychologist had told her that she had a vivid imagination and she lived through her dreams. She subconsciously concocted for herself the most futile and dangerous adventures. Her mind deliberately created extreme situations so as to test her and get her in touch with her true emotions.

She had recurring dreams of lions chasing her in the backwaters of some god-forsaken country, of her being trapped in a roomful of snarling snakes and lizards, of her falling down a steep hill in a speeding car. This was when her past forgave her and did not return to irk her.

Sometimes, she thought she was really insane.

Chapter 4
THE FIRST ACQUAINTANCE

As the lift reached the 2nd floor of the posh, office complex, Faith Jones felt indestructible.

Surprisingly, she was never nervous at job interviews or first days at work. She thrived on change and invited it with open arms. This had been one trait that had shone through in her interview with the Quality Leader as well as the Master Black Belt. Although she was young for the Quality Manager role, the leadership had found her the ideal person for it in terms of maturity as well as grit and assertiveness.

She had been anxious the previous day but after re-assessing her emotions today, while she walked past the buzzing "shop floor", she knew for certain that that feeling had only emerged because of her discomfort over meeting her psychologist for the first time.

A "shop floor" is a terminology used for the area where all the action happens. At any point in time, one can see busybodies pouring over the computer screens and typing away details of people's lives, their medical details, family histories, financial records, investment details.

One of the doors of a small meeting room was open and, as Faith walked by, she casually glanced in to notice a group of intense looking suits, huddled over a round table, engrossed in a serious discussion.

The place was swarming with people. In some bays, one can hear phones ringing and people with headsets chatting in their phony accents to customers in the US or the UK. At least, to Faith, it seemed like chatting. But, she later learned that these agents were resolving complex customer queries on whether their claims had been processed or whether our databases reflected their correct policy status.

It amazed Faith to see the power that agents working on these floors had over the lives of people sitting thousands of miles across the oceans and the seas. She didn't think that neither party realized what was truly at stake.

An agent was being paid only a meager sum of money each month to work 10-12 hours a day, at times, to data enter similar information over and over again, information that was critical enough that it could change a person's future. Faith wondered what could possibly motivate this lot to consistently perform with the same passion and intensity that they probably had when they walked onto this shop floor for the first time. Faith also thought whether other new entrants perhaps a couple of months later would wonder the same about her.

She, however, quickly brushed that thought away. She had to succeed here and prove to herself, more than anyone that she could excel and she knew that she would!

There was a lot of activity on the floor and the atmosphere was charged and Faith quite liked the place once she put away her preliminary reservations.

Business Process Outsourcing was the 'in' thing and Gurgaon was booming with a lot of US companies off-shoring all or some of their processes to be remotely "*run*" in India.

Stan Inc was one such organization, which was into the business of providing Global Outsourcing Solutions to its customers worldwide. It had a setup of over five thousand employees in India alone, catering to its international clientele!

As Faith rounded off her short walk to the end of the floor, she saw her dotted line boss Surinder Kumar coming out of his cabin. His tall, well built physique portrayed a sense of authority about him. He was a man used to giving directions and liked being in charge!

He extended his hand to welcome her as he saw her. She felt a little better and smiled at him in greeting. "Hi, Surinder. I'm really glad to begin my stint with Stan. I look forward to working with you."

"Yes, yes. I hope you bring a lot of external perspective into our operations management. I'm expecting you to use what you have learnt at your MBA at the Indian School of Business. How was the course by the way?"

"It was great, really experiential! A lot of the course work was case study based. But, I think the biggest value add was in the interactions we had on campus with the other students and the professors. The cumulative experience was tremendous and what a lot of us took with us were all the contacts we made."

"Ok. Well, we are currently going through a *fire* situation here. The customer has asked us to ramp-up and we need to hire around 100 underwriters and quick. I was just on my way to a meeting on this. Look, I'll talk to you later. In the meantime, get a good handover from our black belt, Manoj. He is currently working on BPMS for the underwriting process. Get tuned to that immediately. Oh, and he has also closed the RCA for the recent spat of errors in the data entry process. You should get on board with that too. You might need to pitch it out in his absence. He has been such an asset to this process that I am sorry to lose him at this time."

"Sure! Definitely, and I assure you that I will try my level best to pick up the lose ends as quickly as possible."

"Ok." And he turned and walked off. And as he did, Faith felt her bubble deflate a bit.

She had hoped for a much more enthusiastic welcome from Surinder. After all, she would be indirectly reporting in to him. Also, this was her first day and already she felt like there were these huge expectations from her, who knew nothing about the business and absolutely zilch about her role!

The role of a Quality Manager, also called a Black Belt, is a little unstructured that way. And a lot of external hires have never dabbled with quality tools, or six-sigma, before. So, when they hear people talk about Paretos, RCAs, FMEAs, they reach their wits end and pretty fast. And these are just the bare basics!!

"Oh! Dear God!! Let's take a couple of deep breaths, shall we, and figure out who the hell is Manoj and where he sits?" thought Faith as she tried to calm herself a little bit. But then she remembered that she had been told that there would be a 1-month training roadmap to get her up to speed. "Great! I'll find Manoj and figure out how to get trained, quickly."

Surinder who was an Assistant Vice President managed a team of about eight hundred associates who did data entry and underwriting for a US based client, Classic Mortgage Co. Also referred to as CMort, it is one of the major providers of Mortgage insurance in the US. CMort was also one of the largest clients for Stan Inc. and, thus, a very critical account.

The business processing was done in the following manner. The Scanning Team based in the USA, scanned the Mortgage application forms and sent it to India in the form of images. The team here downloaded these images into their Computers with the help of huge servers that were set up in India. The India Operations Team data-entered the applicant's details from the scanned images into data capture screens. In the case of underwriting, critical decisions on whether an applicant should be issued a policy or not were made basis their medical history, demographics and a lot of other criteria.

The team performance was measured against client-defined targets on 2 critical metrics, accuracy and timeliness.

The process was divided into seven teams of around hundred and twenty associates, each managed by a manager and six team leaders. The core team was referred to as 'Operations' as they were responsible for all the operational aspects for this process like ensuring we meet our targets and they get on with the actual running of the process. Experts from the Quality, Human Resource and Training departments, in turn, supported the Operations team.

Faith considered her next course of action for finding Manoj and thought she would be resourceful and, thus, went about the floor in search for him. After asking multiple people and receiving non-committal answers, she realized he was nowhere to be found.

Finally, a short, cute looking woman in a "*mod*" salwar kurta walked up to Faith. By that time, Faith was feeling utterly lost.

"Hi! Are you coming in place of Manoj? You are Faith, right?"

"Hi. Yes, that's quite right. And you are?"

Putting out her hand, she said "I'm Anita. I am an Assistant Manager and I look at one of the data entry processes. I saw you talking to Surinder a short while back. You were looking for Manoj? He hasn't come in yet. I have his mobile number. Why don't you call him and ask him when he would so that you can meet him then?"

"That's a great idea! Thanks", said Faith as she shook Anita's hand. It was a weak handshake but, hey! Anita was a godsend. Faith pulled out her phone to make the crucial call.

"Wow. That's a cool cell. I've never seen one like that before. It looks pretty stylish with the top cover."

It took a moment for Faith to figure out that Anita was indeed talking about her mobile. She had always related a *cell* to Eveready batteries.

"Yeah. Thanks. I always get flip tops. So, what's his number then?"

Manoj seemed to be in a hurry to cut the call but Faith managed to get a feel from him that he would be coming in shortly but only for some time. And in that, he hoped to give her whatever direction he could. "Man! I wish I were the one who had resigned. You can come and go as you wish."

"You bet. But, it's pretty flexible for Black Belts too. Have you met any of the other managers? Also, hasn't Paul come over to introduce you to everyone?"

Paul was the Quality Assistant Vice President, also called the Master Black. He was a Parsi, 31 years old and, to a lot of the young associates in Stan Inc., an extremely handsome hunk. To Faith, however, he was the one who had hired her and given rave reviews about her to HR. To Faith, therefore, he was a mentor she could look up to and respect for his exceptional skill in spotting talent.

"Well, he introduced me to Surinder when I had come in earlier to collect my appointment letter. Today, I was supposed to meet Surinder and speak to him directly. But, I suppose he's really busy today and had to rush to a meeting."

"Oh yes! Surinder is so busy nowadays", Anita said animatedly. "He is such a good Operational Leader! You'll really love working for him. I have been with him for the last 2 years and it has been great!"

"Let's hope so. I do look forward to learning from him."

"Well. Let me introduce you to someone who you would be working with closely. She is a Manager with CMort," said Anita as she guided Faith over to the other extreme of the floor.

"Sure, lets go", she replied. Faith hoped that this manager too would be equally supportive as the other managers she had met today.

As they walked towards the other side of the Shop floor, suddenly Faith had an uneasy feeling. Her feet became heavy and she realized that her habitual brisk walk had somewhat slowed down. Her steps too had become shorter. It was as if there was something stopping her. All her enthusiasm vanished as they approached Bay-3.

Incidentally three was Faith's unlucky number.

"Oh! It seems she hasn't come in yet. Oh, I remember now, she called in."

Just then Faith got a call on her mobile.

"What! Who are you, again? Are you absolutely sure? Black Optra. Yes, that's the no. How bad is it? I'm coming down." It seemed like Faith was hyperventilating.

Suddenly, much to Anita's amusement, Faith sprinted towards the stairs. And as she did, she half-turned back and said in the most surprisingly low, composed voice, "Some son of a gun's banged into my goddamn car."

Those inflammatory words seemed otherworldly when said in that seemingly calm voice especially under the circumstances. Anita was intrigued by Faith and wanted to know how Faith would handle the situation. More likely, how she would "mis"handle the person who had hit her car. So, she followed Faith down to the parking lot.

✤✤✤

'What! Eight hundred applications! How is that possible?' Naina questioned. She was busy discussing the day's unexpectedly high inflow of volumes with her team leader.

'Okay, okay... I'll be there in fifteen minutes,' she assured him. 'Handle it till then. The team will have to stretch to at least a 10 hour day today.' she instructed.

Naina looked at her watch. 'Today will be such a challenge. I am so late', she murmured as she glanced, at the jammed road ahead, in frustration.

It was peak hour in the evening and the roads were buzzing with office traffic. 'People are returning home from work,' she thought. 'Tired and looking forward to a lazy evening or a relaxing bath followed by hot dinner and hours of nonsensical sitcom viewing.'

Naina's day, however, was just beginning.

The BPO industry had taken India by storm. It was a boon for the country. Suddenly, the youth of today had a plethora of opportunities that increased their disposable incomes multiple folds. In return, this industry asked for one small favour, their sleep.

To cater to the US economy they had to work at nights, which took a great deal of telling their bodies that breakfast meant goodnight and a midnight snack, a light lunch.

It was a challenging career choice but rewarding, nonetheless, and Naina loved it.

However, right now her mind was already contemplating the actions needed to take care of this sudden "*fire*" situation at work.

The car entered the office compound and screeched to a halt near the main gate. Naina almost jumped out and starting climbing up the steps, two at a go! It was quite a feat what with her Laptop hanging off one shoulder, her purse off the other and about a dozen books that she had bought for her team members balancing precariously in her hands.

'Hey Naina!' Someone called out to her as she started at the last leg of stairs.

It was Atul, one of the managers from the 'Retirals Team', which was another, big Insurance account at Stan. They had met during a 'Best Practice' Session couple of years back.

In a Best Practice Meet, managers from various businesses share some of the key initiatives that are being driven in their respective shops. This forum is a successful platform to create visibility for their businesses as well a medium to share ideas. Atul and Naina had attended many such sessions together and had hit off well!

As she turned back to steal a quick smile at him, she didn't realize that she had reached the door to the floor and was blocking the exit. Suddenly, the door pushed open to hit her square on the face. Needless to say, the impact of the door on her nose did not feel pleasant.

'I'm sorry.' she heard a soft, yet urgent voice of someone who was already running down the stairs, past her.

The lady looked back up at Naina and asked, 'Do you need help?' She looked rushed and was certainly in a hurry.

Naina was very angry now. All her books were lying scattered while she was holding her face for fear that it may follow suit, all 'cuz of this woman who could not watch her step and she couldn't even help her pick up her bearings without being asked? No. It's obvious you're in a hurry", she replied sarcastically, with an irritated look on her face.

The woman shrugged at that and kept going on.

Just then, Naina noticed a familiar face smirking and sheepishly peeking from behind the door. "Hello, lady! Bad day so far?"

"Hazard a guess, Anita! That woman! What gall she had! A clear case of hit and run! I should be allowed to sue her. Whatcha say? It's like asking a run over pedestrian if he'd like a ride to the hospital!"

That likening made Anita grin even more. And seeing her smile, Naina broke into one herself. This silly incident had set her so mad! And then, as she began to chat with Anita about the latest production update, she rounded up her belongings.

In all this chaos, she ignored the silent nagging of her heart. "Do you remember that lady? It is she!"

❧❧❧

Faith ran to the spot where she had parked her car. As soon as she saw her originally magnificent, perfectly cared for, sedan, she lost it!

This piece of machine had always meant so much more to her than just a means of transport. It signified freedom, independence both financial as well as emotional. This car had heart! It ran like a dream and when Faith sat in the driver's seat, the car enveloped her and protected her so she felt that "nuthin' could do her no harm". It was her comfort blanket when she needed a hug. The fact that it was a beauty attracted Faith to it much more! Although it sounds cliché but Faith called it her "Black Beauty". This was as silly as Faith let herself get.

The rear was completely disfigured. There was a huge dent where there once was the beautiful bumper and the trunk. The backlights were littered on the ground in shards of glass, and the number plate… "Well… what do I do with this now?" Faith panicking internally as she picked it up. The car was in such a mess.

Faith went to the security room and asked for an explanation from the security personnel. "Who the hell did this to my car?" she demanded to know. "We do not know, madam. One of our guards saw the car in this condition and informed us."

"How can you not know? What are you all here for? What do you get paid for? Please explain why no one immediately responded to the deafening alarm that my car was sounding and caught that ****hole* before he could pick up his tail between his legs and run! Did someone even see who it was or which car he drove?" She snarled at them.

"Madam, one of the guards said it was a red Zen and a lady was trying to park it but when it hit your car she drove away. She could have parked it anywhere on the road and we will not be able to find it now"

"Well, that's perfect! Thanks for all your help" she called out sarcastically as she turned to enter the office building again.

Looking at their nonplussed faces, she had realized that her anger was misplaced and arguing would reap worthless rewards. Even her sarcasm was lost on them. It had helped displace some of her nervous energy but just enough so that she did not feel guilty for it.

The damage was done but she was not. She had to go back to work and meet the work shirker, Manoj, and the operations manager who had no concept of turning to work on time.

It was turning out to be Faith's worst day… well, maybe not the worst, but it sure was in the running for it!

✾✾✾

Naina was busy instructing her team leaders to re-assign applications. She had gone for a brief meeting with the, "missing in action" but now present, but in a tearing hurry to leave, black belt, Manoj, who had suggested a few action steps.

The application flow was high and they had to request for help from another process to lend their cross- trained resources to pool in. She suggested that Team Leads themselves process applications too.

Finally, she returned back to her desk and sat down. She picked up one of the books she had recently bought and smiled. 'Fish' was one of her favorite management books, so engrossing and full of natural wisdom. So simple yet it taught management's most important and publicized concepts yet the least understood: Passion@ work. It is a must for all to read.

As Naina's computer beeped her to log in, she looked up from her book and caught the same rude woman walking to Anita's desk.

"Who is she? I've never seen her around. How does she know Anita?"

She noticed her in serious conversation with Anita for a while. And then Anita pointed towards the end of Naina's bay. She was pointing to her seat!

"Oh! Maybe she wants to find me to apologize for earlier. About time!"

A flicker of recognition crossed Naina's mind as she studied her… and then some more as she walked over to her seat.

Quickly, Naina turned to look into her computer screen to seem occupied. "Shit! It's still logging me on. Where's my book?" And then, she pretended to read.

"Naina Chopra?"

"That's me."

"Do you, by any chance, drive a red Zen?"

"What is it to you? And yes, I do."

"One more question, if I may? Are you a learner?"

"Yes, Miss Interrogation! May I ask what your problem is?"

And this was when all hell broke loose.

"My problem is that irresponsible neurotics like you drive when you don't know which leg to put on which side of the gear!" shouted Faith.

"My car is smashed beyond repair and you sit here reading "Fish"! If you don't know how to drive, then why do you take chances with other people's lives and property?"

Faith was at the point of no return. She kept lecturing till she had almost run out of breath and her face had attained a weird reddish-blue tint. She finally pointed a finger at Naina and said, "You make this right. You hear me?" At that, she stomped out.

Naina was zapped. For once, she was at a loss of words. She didn't know what had hit her! Embarrassed and shocked, she looked around. Luckily, her team was in an updates' huddle. She looked down at the book in her hands. It felt heavy ... it was just a 100 pager.

Naina was a true Aquarian. Like the water bearer that she was, she needed tranquility and peace of mind to feel truly happy. Although, she enjoyed her long unending debates on mundane topics of general living, she hated altercations. Her mind realized that this woman who had just scolded her had just had her car run into and was obviously under a gross misunderstanding, but her heart just wanted to lash out at her.

She then slowly put down the book at which she had been blankly staring at all this while, got up a little unsteadily and hurried to the rest room, as best her shaky legs could carry her. Her eyes were misty.

✾✾✾

Faith didn't know where to go next. She was fuming and living her nightmare: It was her first day at work, she had achieved nothing that she would've liked to so far and she had already picked up a fight with the guards and a manager who would, in all probability, be critical in her future success. To top it all, she now felt guilty at losing her temper to the extent she did.

So, as she went back to the stairs to think through her next steps, this is what she ended up thinking.

"This is just great, Faith! You have done it again. Best of luck trying to get out of this one!"

That Faith had extremely bad luck was beyond question. That Faith handled her bad luck worse was inevitable.

Faith's head was heavy now and she could feel the tension seep through her. Determined still to make something of her day, Faith decided to find Manoj, if he had managed to make an appearance.

As she hit the floor again, she heard someone call her name. She turned to meet a short, balding man probably in his early 30s running up to meet her.

"Hi. I'm Manoj. Anita pointed you out to me. I caught you, just in time. I need to leave in half an hour."

"Hi. Ok. Well, then I'd appreciate whatever you can start me on today. Will you be coming in tomorrow?"

"Yes. I'll spend some more time with you tomorrow. Have you met the others?"

"Well... they're in a meeting, I think. And I could've done without my meeting with Naina."

"Why? What happened?"

"Her car rammed into mine's what happened. I lost it with her." Faith replied, now with her anger a little under control.

"Hey! There's gotta be somethin' amiss here. She came in the office cab tonight, with me. That's why we both got a little late"

"Thank you, Lord! This day just keeps getting better!" Faith moaned louder than she intended as she hailed to an imaginary God floating on the false ceiling overhead.

"Do you mind if we just sit tomorrow?" Faith requested. "I must correct this, if I can. And thanks for that. This is a huge misunderstanding".

"Hey, cool! No probs. I'll see ya tomorrow. Best of luck", said Manoj with a smile and a wave.

Waving back, Faith ran back to find Naina.

***

Naina was having trouble keeping those tears back when she reached the comfort of the empty restroom.

She cried freely for a while, thinking what had transpired. And then it clicked!

"I saw her at the market yesterday, with the puppy!"

Naina was now intrigued more than ever. Her curious streak was getting the better of her. She wanted to go and speak with this woman. Although she was still angry, the primary thought of revenge had dissipated soon, too soon for Naina.

Naina ordinarily killed incidents and memories through detailed post-mortems. She then tortured the offenders with muted indifference. But, here, she just wanted to know more about this person. She even admired the way she had faced Naina, and totally incapacitated her with her words.

Naina would never have been able to do that had she been in those shoes. Although Naina was ambitious, strong and ordinarily chatty, under duress, she clammed up.

Naina stared at her reflection in the mirror. Her eyes were puffy already and quite red. She had the kind of face that could not hide.

"Gosh. How can I go out looking like this? Get a grip, Naina. The team needs you on the floor right now."

She still took her time rounding up and stepped out attaining a measure of her original composure.

And then she flinched. "Oh No! Not again".

Walking towards her was the woman of the hour. Her stride was still confident and she was looking right at Naina. Naina wondered if she was coming for a re-take or a double whammy. Squaring her shoulders and standing tall, Naina readied herself for an onslaught this time, knowing all the while who would win that duel!

"Hi", she heard and blinked to replay that in her mind's memory. Whoa! Whazzat?

"May I speak to you on what happened earlier? Look, I know it wasn't you, now. And you must've realized that I was under a misconception. Why didn't you say anything?"

Naina was completely bewildered on hearing this.

"Who are you, by the way?"

"I'm Faith. I've joined in place of Manoj."

At this, Naina's mind was playing at so many angles that she could not think clearly. And then, she uttered in her soft, melodious voice and a little too mildly for her liking, "What the hell kind of an apology is this?"

"It's been a crazy day for me. And then this car mishap happens to completely whack me out. How did you imagine I would talk to someone who's responsible for the most part? Also, now I'm reeling from guilt because you couldn't interject before I made a complete idiot out of myself. How would you react when all this happens on top of your worst day?"

Naina could see the logic in all this, albeit dwarfed. But it was still a sorry attempt at a sorry. All this while, Faith was carrying on about the fact that she did not mean to be mean to someone who did not really deserve it and yadda, yadda, yadda. In spite of herself, Naina's mouth lifted at the sides in a half-smile. Faith was such a funny character, she thought. Although anyone else would have felt otherwise, Naina already understood her. She could not deny the connection here.

Finally, Faith muttered, almost under her breath and barely audible. Naina almost missed it.

"I'm sorry, OK. I am ordinarily not this rude. But, I was mad! And I would do it again."

There you go, Naina thought. That wasn't so tough, although, she could've done without the "do it again" bit.

Faith had rambled on for some time now and was now dragging in long breaths to re-oxygenate her body. She was also waiting for Naina to come out of her reverie.

Naina suddenly looked up to meet Faith's eyes and then spoke for the third time since they'd met.

"Wanna have some Coffee? "

Naina smiled.

❀❀❀

They sat comfortably on the not so comfortable chairs sipping cold coffee at the barista counter in the cafeteria.

They talked about themselves, their professional experiences and hobbies. They did that for quite a while, a good half-day's work worth a' while! And an unexpected development began to take shape. Faith started to like Naina.

Naina asked Faith how she came to be here and Faith took her through more of the story than she had intended to. How she had wanted to prove that she could make a difference in a man's world. How a lot of who she was and what she did was to try and prove that she belonged.

It was a couple of hours of chitchat before Naina glanced at her watch and cried out.

'My God, we've been sitting here for almost two hours!' I just did not realize the time, she exclaimed.

'Yaa, its been long. I could never have imagined that you could talk so much', Faith laughed as she teased Naina.

'*Theek hai Theek hai*, its your day today. Tomorrow will be mine', Naina joined the laughter.

Though it had been a little difficult at first for Faith to break the ice, she got very comfortable as Naina put her at ease by deliberately ignoring the events that had taken place few hours ago between them.

They talked about various topics in general and in between Naina told Faith about herself and her small world that revolved around the two men that had conquered her life...her husband Yash and her dog Randy.

They discovered a few startling things they had in common.

'I love reading, painting and eating out, not necessarily in the same order', Naina mocked.

'Wow! Me too', Faith replied.

They both enjoyed painting although their styles like their personalities were diametrically divergent.

Faith was traditional in her approach and put extensive research of classical arts behind her works. She had traveled to Paris only to spend a week studying the unparalleled collection of art at the Louvre. She worked on reproductions of famous paintings and artists of the Dutch era as well as the more prominent ones like Turner and Rembrandt.

Naina worked on her instincts and discovered original abstracts; mirages of shadows, myriad textures and colors blended in to recreate a personal moment in time, an emotion or a special memory.

Faith, on the other hand, always worked off others'.

Faith was quite impressed when Naina told her that she was associated with a Blind School and donated her time and all the money that she made by selling off her paintings to the school.

Both of them also had had unconventional families and the hard, cold hand of fate had marked their childhoods.

Faith opened up to Naina telling her about her past and the fact that she lost both her parents early. Growing up had not been easy for Faith, as the empty void could never be filled. And then, as if it wasn't enough, Rohan came into her life and spoilt it. She'd met him through a chat session on the Internet and before they both realized, he had proposed and she had said yes.

'It was a bad relationship and shortly we both learnt that it would not work, so we ended it,' Faith stated.

'It lasted for seven months'.

It all seemed a jig jaw puzzle to Naina with some blank spots in between. What she had just learnt about Faith had posed a lot of questions in her mind. She was intrigued to know more but she did not ask Faith.

'Howz work here', she asked Naina.

'You know Faith, in a typical operations setup specially ours, one doesn't know what all lies ahead, as the day moves on. We have to face so many challenges in a day that it kind of becomes easy. You solve one problem and another one crops up. Its crazy! And in the midst of all this, there's this one call or one appreciation mail from the customer that brightens up your day and once again you get charged up to do more', Naina's eyes lit up as she said this.

'The environment is so bloody dynamic that the only thing that's permanent here is change. And change is always good as it give you a lot of exposure. That's the beauty of this industry!' She added proudly.

Faith observed that Naina had a relatively easy way of describing things and she used her hand movements a lot to support her words.

'Hmmm...Sounds quite interesting', Faith replied.

There always comes a time in conversations, especially with fresh acquaintances when you suddenly run out of chitchat. But that never happened with them. Or at least they did not take notice. When a warm silence did at last fall over them, they both thought the very same thing, that they were simply having fun. And the "process fires", lives' little emergencies, crazy first days, all for some moments seemed a million miles away.

'*Chalo*, lets make a move, I've got to reach home before midnight to get up early in the morning and give the car for repair', Faith suggested.

'Cool. See ya tomorrow. I'd better get back to the shop floor. I am surprised no one's missed me till now!' Naina muttered.

'I am glad to have set this right with Naina" Faith though as she drove back home in her battered car.

It was a while before Naina got the chance to take a break. She had attended several meetings, one of which had not gone well. She was exhausted by the end of it and as she sat down on her desk, her mind was filled with thoughts of Faith. She had liked her in spite of her erratic behavior tonite. 'Interesting woman', Naina though. 'I'd like to know her better'.

This is how a very important phase in both their lives began. And like most important moments in people's lives, they did not comprehend, at the time, its *true* import.

Mostly, it's the little things that strengthen the ties of a friendship. For Faith, it was Naina bypassing the embarrassing subject of Faith's misplaced outrage at her. This, she thought, was considerate of Naina, and the not-so-brief encounter at the office Barista counter with Naina had a surprisingly disarming effect on her. She quickly relaxed and began to mirror Naina's easy personal style and mannerisms.

Naina recognized that this meeting had only reaffirmed her initial premonition that this was someone that she was meant to be friends with, and definitely someone she now liked to be with. She felt something happening, something that hadn't happened in a long time, that she desperately longed for… for a long time

She felt connected.

PART TWO

FAITH 'S FOLLY

The next two weeks passed in a blur. Faith made do with a lousy handover from a very blasé Manoj.

Surinder, Faith realized, had it in for her… probably institutional competition. He hailed from one of the most prestigious MBA institutes in the country, but still no comparison to the internationally acclaimed and backed ISB. He was intent to prove that Faith was a miss-hire and incompetent to handle the role she had been handed. He used every meeting, discussion, one on one, to try and discredit everything Faith tried to achieve in spite of no help from any of the other managers.

Surinder promoted unhealthy competition between the many managers under him. He prided himself in discontent and even enmity between them. This, he rationalized, would keep people on their toes, they would put in twice the hours they ordinarily would, push themselves to the edge and achieve thrice as much. As expected, CMort was on the brink of being pulled back. The process accuracy for the Underwriting process was just bordering around the target and Faith wanted to do a project to improve that. But, Surinder had his way and the project was scrapped even before it began.

Naina was on good terms with Surinder, all the other managers were. Faith, however, was more perceptive than Naina and knew that the *bon homme* image was a façade and that Surinder had the potential to turn hostile when it would suit his needs.

As if this were not enough, there seemed to be a collusion bubbling. From the first interaction, most people at Stan Inc. had taken a wary stand with Faith. They wanted to believe that she was cutthroat ambitious and would do better than them, even though they had seen no evidence of it yet. But the fancy black sedan she drove and the fancier top-notch apartment complex she lived in urged them to want to dislike her.

In the midst of all this mayhem, Naina and Faith continued to de-stress in each other's company at every opportunity they could create.

One late night, when they were hob-knobbing over delicious Chinese food, Naina's favorite, she warned Faith.

As Naina nibbled on a rather moist, succulent chicken dim sum, she told her that the fact that she drove the car that she did, while her boss's boss came in a measly Zen, would give rise to bruised egos and backlashes.

A frown marred the alabaster smoothness of Faith's brow.

"Babe, I don't buy this bit of reasoning for all the nonsense I've been put through. I don't have an assigned workstation; they have not yet given me a laptop. Ordinarily, Black Belts get those basics on the first day they hit the floor. Surinder does not acknowledge my presence and I am happier when he doesn't 'cuz I don't care for his attitude when he does." Faith took a short rasp of a breath before carrying on.

"If they want to act childish about this, so will I!! I will go back to Paul and tell him what I think about this stupid role, this god-forsaken process and he can take it all and shove it. I don't need this. I have been taking Surinder's rude abruptions for the last 2 weeks. Already, coming in to work has become a burden. What is to become of me if things continue as they are? The bugger won't listen to me! And now, you tell me that the car I drive, of which I cannot do anything, by the way, is the root of it. You know how insane all this sounds? I've worked before. Never have I faced this sort of idiocracy."

Naina knew what Faith was going through. She had been in many of those meetings when Surinder deliberately negated Faith's inputs or abruptly cut her sentences mid-way. But listening to Faith ramble on so passionately about this in that silly brit accent, Naina smiled in spite of herself.

"Listen. Why don't you try coming in the cab for some time?" Naina suggested.

"I did that, remember? When my car was in the shop, I did that! Anyhow, if you really think this is the reason of it all, then perceptions have already been drawn and no good will come of putting myself through further misery by breaking my back in those dreaded cabs"

Naina was convinced that Faith would not budge and she could not counter her hard logic and reasoning. Yes, if it had to be this way then so shall it. They could fight it… they would find a way.

In the meantime, there were bigger forces at work.

✤✤✤

With the advent of technological distractions, the youth of today have succumbed to the faster and less messy routes to communication. Whether it is inviting people to a social gathering or wishing someone on one of the many Indian festivals and, most so, for apologizing for a misdeed, a quick SMS does the trick.

Faith had often been guilty of it herself. Not to say she was proud of it but what better way to keep the gates of communication open without, literally, lifting a finger or two.

Faith ruefully acknowledged to her that the art of conversation was indeed dying. Being a Libran, she personally liked her intermittent doses of intellectual discussions or, for that matter, any good ol' topic that she could argue both sides of. But, due to lack of the right company and her guarded nature, she seldom indulged in the practice, which is ordinarily a Libran's bane of survival itself.

With Naina, though, Faith made that extra effort… probably 'cause Naina made her. She has this uncanny capacity to carry on a conversation all by herself. And that probably made Faith ride over and beyond her reserved disposition with relative ease.

Now, that's not to say that Faith was not an open person. Nothing could be further from the truth. She may not reveal much about her private life on her own accord yet she has tremendous potential to shock, with blatant matter-of-factness, if asked specific questions.

Naina and Faith saw a demonstration of this trait around a month post their fateful tête a tête over coffee. They were chatting with Anita in one of the office building's more obscure meeting rooms.

Anita, as you might remember, and, as they later found out, was the one who had deliberately lied to Faith about Naina crashing into her precious car. In any case, Anita was excellent at clawing into people's lives and finding residence in their minds. She would then plant seeds of venomous vines and sit back and gleefully observe them go to work! Meanwhile, Faith had gotten fairly comfortable with her constant chatter and long renderings of "who said what to whom" and other mischievous office gossip.

Faith was not really much of a gossipmonger, or so she'd have liked to believe, but she reasoned that it pays to listen to one especially if you are the new kid on the block. And she was, literally, the youngest manager in the division.

Faith prided herself on her maturity and intellect, however, every once in a while the best of us end up making mistakes. This one, she later realized to her detriment, spurred on more problems than she could have accounted for.

A simple question, an open, though played down, answer later, the triplet were talking about her broken engagement with Rohan and what a madman he had been. The discussion then led towards her residence with his family in London for thc majority of 2001.

The tides of life had taken a considerable dip in that year for her. But she had never shied away from staring back at those miserable memories straight in the eyes and inhaling them to the core of her heart, if only to re-learn the lessons of the past.

Unfortunately, that short exchange of facts, and they were mere facts to her as she relayed them with much emotional detachment, caught Anita's attention.

✽✽✽

A month had passed in faith's new job at stan inc. And things hadn't started looking up yet.

Black Belts are supposed to complete a roadmap in the first 18-24 months of their role in which they need to undergo a 3 weeks comprehensive training on the six sigma methodology and quality tools that they would then need to test for and apply on at least 2 high impact quality projects, which would need to yield excellent benefits and assist the core metrics, for the processes they are aligned to, to reach entitlement.

With a month gone and not much achieved, Faith was getting restless. She had not been nominated for the trainings yet and each project idea she had submitted to Surinder, more humbly than she had intended to, had been showed the door. What was most bugging was that Surinder would let her do the entire groundwork for the first stage of the project and then, just as that flicker of hope reemerged, he would pull the plug on it.

Faith was an ordinarily competitive person but had never been ambitious from a professional aspect. Contrary to popular belief, all she had dreamed of her entire life was to find her Prince Charming and marry him, cook for him and raise his children. In India, a vast majority of city raised, well-educated girls from established families still harbor this fantasy. And, regretfully, for a majority of them, it remains just that, *a fantasy*.

For Faith had learnt, through a debilitating and painful experience, that marriage was far from "living happily every after" and that Prince Charming was a toad!

On a scorching August afternoon, she settled in a sink-in Swede chaise lounge in the comfort of her stylishly decorated bedroom. She looked out at the lush, manicured greens and deceptively cooling fountains of her residential complex. This room, especially, was her favorite in the house as it also housed all the memories of her life so far. She had stylish taste and had elegantly restored old furniture to its former glory and created a study cum bedroom. With wood paneled walls to house an expansive collection of books to old, Turkish carpets to beautiful oil landscapes and portraits, and a pretty sandalwood *mandir* on one end, this room looked like something out of an art deco book.

She had even built a special peep-in cabinet which showed off memories from the past like cute little gifts she had received on her birthdays, farewell cards, collectibles from her trips abroad, snaps and the lot.

In contrast to a very male study concept, she had strategically set, in the center of the room, a four-post queen sized bed with the frills. Long trails of muslin in cool shades of pink and earthy colors hung from the posts down to the parquet flooring. Soft, feather filled, pillows in the same hues added to the feminine feel.

Faith looked around her and took in every corner and element of the room. She admired this room and what it stood for. This room represented Faith for she was duality personified. She had the physical stamina and confidence of a man but the loyalty, emotional strength and courage of a woman.

Her eye caught a sudden movement behind the half shut door. Reflexively, she bolted up only to find a sheepish look from her newfound love as he peeped in from behind the door.

She had come to adore him over the short time they had lived together, just about a month actually. Faith, who hated limiting her independence, had taken solace in his presence and grown overtly accustomed to it. Now, she could not imagine her afternoons without him waking her up with a wet kiss on her lips or the time they spent on their morning walks together or that finally she had a special someone waiting up for her when she got back from work.

She called him Fuzzy because he was a hairy little monster but more so due to the fact that Faith really was uncertain why she got him home with her that afternoon at the shrink or what was the purpose of her finding him on the road, injured and whimpering. All she knew was what she felt about him, the rest was fuzzy and that's how she wanted it, forever.

"Hi, my sleepy baby! My cutie pie... my darling little toy monsta! Come 'eere to didi… come come, silly doddy boy! Awww, look at you all wobbly and tumbly", Faith murmured as Fuzzy made his uncertain and unsteady way through her room to where she was now bending low to pick him in her arms when he joined her.

"That's it. You're all cozy and safe now, aren't you? Aren't you, my puppy" Faith was crazy about him and he was a sweetheart.

He was still limping a bit from his recent accident but the vet had reaffirmed at each of the dozen odd calls Faith had made over the last month that he would be absolutely fine relatively soon. She was desperately praying for that day. Like anybody who loves another living being, she wanted the best for Fuzzy and she was determined to make it happen.

Faith continued with her reading while Fuzzy found his comfort spot in her lap and nuzzled his tiny face against her forearm, licking imaginary milk toffees up her arm with carefree abandon.

She had picked up a spiritually telling book by Dr. Brian Weiss, a psychologist (a coincidence?) turned spiritualist who wrote about his patient's as well as his enlightening, life-altering experiences with Regression and Progression Therapy.

"*Many Lives Many Masters*" was about a woman named Catherine who had been fighting her many phobias all her life before she came to Brian for help. When nothing worked with her, Brian ventured deeper into regression techniques and started using them on her for hope of some results. The results startled them because, over time, not only did they get rid of her phobias, they really understood the reason for them. They were remnants of her previous lifetimes.

The other discovery made by Brian changed the course of his life and those of millions. "*The Masters*", as he calls them, are really higher order spirits who answered for him the eternal questions, "Why are we here?" and more importantly, "What are we and how should we live our lives?" Faith was amazed as she went through more. She had, over the years, formed a concept in her heart for the very same questions. Doesn't everybody? When this book and "The Masters" reaffirmed so much, she took solace and so much comfort in that. So many things started to fit for her and she immediately became more relaxed.

Multiple lifetimes, kindred spirits featuring as close friends or relatives, period of redemption and study, the white light experience post death, the pragmatic purpose of life, soul mates. It all made sense to Faith. She adopted this ideology as her religion. She needed faith.

There were certain folks whose mere presence tended to make faith ill at ease, inducing the nervous laugh, the fiddling with the pen or notepad and the embarrassed shuffling of the feet.

Mr. Chanchal "Big Shit", as people fondly called him, was heading the Financial Services vertical for Stan Inc. and had been a steady fixture in the company since its inception. People said that it would be fitting if he retired from the same office he had occupied for the last 6 years or so.

Irrespective, he was a man who knew his job well. He was in his late forties, a little mature for the BPO Industry as it is common knowledge that the evil here is a lot of thirty year olds in powerful positions holding ransom hundreds of careers and earning more in a decade than their parents earned in their lifetimes. It takes a day for all this to go to their heads and several lifetimes to come off.

Anyhow, Chanchal was good at what he did. After all, he was a veteran but his management funda was to be so direct and blunt, bordering on rude, that although he demanded respect on his face, he got contempt behind his back.

He reminded Faith of Mr. Burns from "*The Simpsons*" with the thin, wiry frame but packed with a lot of punch, skeletal features and cunning piercing eyes.

Chanchal, to people he took a liking to, was a godsend. He managed their careers for them to certain successdom, ensured they bagged the best roles, and backed them up to Hell and back. All in all, he adopted the lot. He could be as blind as the Lady of Justice and forgive murder for the ones he liked. They could just do no wrong!

Faith, despite her uneasiness, had made a good first impression on Chanchal. Naina had briefed her that this could be the clincher if she wanted to make her career here. But, guess what! Surinder was already in His Majesty's good books and the devil incarnated ensured otherwise. He was "getting at her" from all quarters while she could not put her finger on what she had really done to deserve it.

PART THREE

NAINA

'Naina... Naina', she heard her mom calling out in the distance.

Naina, Naina *beti*... where are you', the voice was coming closer now.

'There you are.'

Naina felt someone sit beside her. She stirred.

'Day dreaming again, my little angel?' She felt her mother's warm hands on her hair, gently stroking them away from her face.

Slowly Naina opened her eyes and smiled.

'Maa, I am soooo hungry. What have you made for lunch'.

'*Rajma Chawal* along with *Boondi Raita*', her mom replied. *Rajma Chawal* was Naina's favorite dish.

'*Chalo* get up. I'll serve dinner.'

'Dinner?'

'Yes, Darling, its 8 o clock at night'

'Have I slept for so long?' she questioned herself. 'Guess, I lost track of time. Anyway it was night for me and my day begins now.'

Just like most people who work, Naina longed for weekends. Thursday was her favorite day as it was just one day away from Saturday!

Whenever Yash was on tour, she spent the weekends at her parents place in Lajpat Nagar.

This weekend too, she had come straight from office on Saturday morning after completing her night shift. She had hit the bed right away and was lost in her dreams until her mom woke her up.

She chatted with her mom for a while before they went off to bed. Naina shared a very special relationship with her mother. The bond between them was strong and, in fact, it had become stronger after Naina's marriage. Their relationship had matured from a mother-daughter's to that of two friends. Naina shared almost everything with her mother.

Almost.

As everything cannot be discussed with parents, specially mothers. They get too worried if their kids are tensed or have a problem.

Finally, when everyone else went off to sleep, she started to surf through the books in her old teakwood bookrack. She still had some books here, though she'd taken most of them with her to Yash's place after marriage.

She found what she was looking for – *Kaleidoscope* by Daniel Steel.

It was a story of three sisters bonded by blood and separated by fate. The eldest of them was the main character named Hillary, who had gone through a very tough life and had struggled to fight and win the odds. Naina could relate herself to Hillary, as she too had been "*blessed*" with a painful childhood and tough youth. Courtesy… her abusive father. Naina had managed to survive and succeed only by sheer hard work and passion.

Naina had read the book multiple times as it had a soothing effect on her. Hillary had inspired her to hold on.

Today, Naina was successful. She had survived …… beautifully.

Naina was an avid and a fast reader and finished the book in a couple of hours.

'What do I do now', she thought.

Something struck her mind and she tiptoed to her mother's bedroom. Slowly, she opened one of the closets and pulled out her Wedding Album.

Her mom treasured it as if it were jewel.

She sat on the cozy couch in the living room and started to turn the pages. Even today, she could replay the entire scenario in her mind. It was crystal clear as if there was a film playing in front of her with all the emotions included!

She giggled as she saw Yash and her smiling faces, fitted in a frame resembling a television, in the photo! Camera tricks could be so funny!

She saw her mother and brother hugging her just before the *Jai Mala*. God! She was crazy about her mother and adored her brother who was three years younger to her.

She turned a couple of pages more and her smile faded as she saw her mother in law along with Yash's elder sister, brother and his hi-tech wife all beaming in the photograph with their recently cleaned canals… all 32 of them each, staring into the camera. It was a picture perfect pose for the '*Close-Up*' ad. Only that no body would buy '*Close-Up*' then!

Yash had told her about his background. However she had not been duly prepared for his family…

Yash belonged to the rich class. Neo-rich and ultra modern class to be precise. Only that all the richness was a show off to maintain their so-called high standards, loading the women of the house with all the jewelry that they possessed, at all times.

And modernization to them meant throwing huge parities in their lavish bungalow or their farmhouse in Sanik Farms. Yash's dad – Manohardas Chopra was a very successful rice exporter. They had factories in Punjab, Ludhiana and Amritsar to be precise. Their rice brand "Noore-Basmati" was very popular in India and abroad. He was a socialite and they invited, to these parties, the who's who in the city. From industrialists to politicians to models, all were a part of this drama. Liquor flowed freely and new liaisons were made. These parties lasted till the wee hours of the morning where people generally came in with someone and left with somebody else.

Yash's mom and his sister-in-law (elder brother's wife) paraded the house will all their *glitter-ables*...round the clock. They even slept with their make up on, just incase there could be a mid-night fire or an earthquake and they would have to run out of the house. They ought to look prim and proper at all times. Although Naina felt it was more because they were scared that their husbands would be shocked to see their real faces!

Naina smiled at this thought. She could never identify herself with them. There was just no connection. This also reminded her of her school days.

Even though it was tough for her mom, she had given her daughter the best education available back then. Naina had gone to one of the most expensive and happening school in town, a school where the cream of the society sent their kids for studying. However, she faced resentment and rejection from many of her class mates, specially the girls. She was smart, intelligent and a topper so they wanted to be her friend. But as soon as they got close to her and got to know about her middle class background, they moved away.

Naina didn't bother either. She had a tomboyish personality with being excellent in sports and had hence won lot of guy friends. They didn't care about where she came from, how much money her parents had... and all that crap. They treated her like one of them and she was quite comfortable in their company.

But it had certainly created a vacuum for a best friend that had never got filled......not till now.

Still she believed life had been fair to her. She had done well in life, had a decent job and a comfortable home with a loving husband and was proud of it. However, she was very grounded and had never let herself forget her roots. This helped her in bonding easily with people and they loved her for it. Naina Chopra was truly a people's person.

❦❦❦

As Faith walked out of the office building towards where the loading for the office cabs takes place (her car had needed to go back to the workshop), she noticed Surinder and Anita in deep conversation. She had ordinarily not heard Surinder talking as much, if not to rebuke her, and, that too, with such interest in the discussion. She was curious to know what was being discussed. She wished, sometimes, that she could get into people's minds and see what they were thinking. This, she registered must be a necessity in order to communicate with Surinder because he apparently expects you to be a mind reader for the most part.

Although she had a dotted line reporting to Surinder, he had not once taken the time to induct her or set expectations in the month she'd been here. Faith still had to go in search of a new seat multiple times during the shift because she had not been allocated a laptop or a permanent seat yet. She had a hunch that things would only get worse… much worse.

She figured it was time to bring her direct boss, Paul, a little more updated on her status with Surinder. He had gotten dismissive of Faith or else extremely rude. "Maybe he can talk some sense into him. I'll speak to him tomorrow afternoon as soon as I come in."

Although she had briefed Paul on her progress earlier, he had only asked her to be more patient. There was apparently a dearth in *this* multinational for laptops! And Paul reasoned that Surinder must've been busy with the many problems plaguing the process, which is why he would have bypassed the expectation setting. And that he probably did not give her work to do because there were already all the other tenured managers begging for handouts from him. "Keep the faith, Faith", Paul had snickered at his silly joke, much to her disgust. "We'll send you for the Black Belt training soon. Then, you'll get more equipped to take on initiatives."

✤✤✤

Faith received a call from naina no sooner than she had pushed open her apartment door, to the likes of Fuzzy bounding up and down, excitedly, yelping happy war cries.

"Hey Nain! Just reached. You still in the cab?"

"Yup. I gotta tell you something I just overheard. Anita and Surinder were talking in the parking lot where the cabs station themselves at drop time. They obviously didn't notice me walking by. So, I generally stood around behind the closest cab. I love it when I'm such a devil" Naina grinned. She carried on, "It's important and explains why Surinder has been acting the way he is"

"Great! I love it too. I noticed them there and was sooo curious to know. Finally, some answers. Come on, Sherlock Holmes, let's hear it."

"I heard him say to Anita that he thinks that ISB is a "pay 10 lakhs and get a degree" kind of institute. It takes a no-brainer to get through and he was always against the MBB and the Quality Leader taking you in. Apparently, there was someone from his institute that he was selling for this very same role. Thus, his need to discredit you, you see! Also, he said and I quote verbatim, "So, she thinks she a big shot, does she? Working as a Black Belt at Stan and driving her expensive car. I will teach her a lesson she will never forget. I will teach her what it is to face someone who has actually had to fight for where he is!" So, there! I feel he had this bone to pick even before he saw you though. But, meeting you would've only added fuel because I feel that he knows subconsciously that you have it in you to do well here."

"Nain, it never occurred to me that people here would be so twisted. I mean, this company is supposed to be a World Class Employer! How can they bear people who take things so personally at literally no provocation? Wait till I'm through with him. Then, he'll really have something to avenge against me!"

"Hey! I just remembered. We have got to be careful of Anita as well now because, just as I left for my own cab, I heard him ask her if she had dug up something on you. In so many words"

"Nain, I will play him and defeat him at his own game. Tooth and nails! No rules. That's how he likes it, doesn't he!"

Naina and Faith talked for another hour drawing up a game plan… that would work real well!

✽✽✽

The next day when faith walked in to work she was a woman on a mission.

She went straight into Paul's cabin; she had set up a meeting with him for this time.

"Yes, madam. *Kya chal raha hai?* What can I do for you?" said he half expecting Faith to start off on another one of her complaining tirades.

Faith turned on her charm; full force ahead! "It's going great, Paul. And you have done so much for me already; I just wanted to thank you for that. Also, I want to update you on my progress." Faith said smiling her sweetest smile. Nobody likes a complaining tiddy dee, right? she thought to herself.

"My pleasure! So, let's hear it." Paul said smiling coyly. Who could resist that smile? He seemed surprised to say the least.

"Well... Naina's quality project is going great guns. We've made a lot of progress over the last month. We're really changing the course of the project and it should not take another 1 year to complete it."

"At the same time, Anita is stalling. She has not worked on hers at all. You know, I have also noted that she is not comfortable with excel, she fibbles with the report outs and needs help with simple tools like Paretos. You know, in the short time that I have worked with Anita, I wonder how Surinder gave her a Top Performer rating!" Faith closed with true amazement in her voice.

"Also, I feel that it's pertinent for you to know that the Underwriting process does not have simple graphs that represent historical and present performance. That's a basic, even I know, that should exist! No wonder that accuracy is a challenge in the area. In the call, the other day, the client was quite livid with this. Do you think this could erupt into a major crisis soon?

"Paul, remember I mentioned those projects Surinder did not feel were required and he scrapped them in the Define Phase? One of them was on the accuracy for this very same process", she stressed the last sentence for impact.

Paul seemed interested, very intrigued. After all, Faith knew he would be. He needed something on Surinder himself, something really big like favoritism, under-performing processes or prejudices. She knew that because she had made it her business to know. There was a position open, a promotion from an AVP position to a VP position in the Insurance Division with only two contenders: Paul and Surinder.

✾✾✾

Faith wondered why she hadn't used Paul earlier to her advantage. She knew why. She wasn't a conniving person nor was she political. But, in one month, she had recognized that she would have to be these and much more in order to make a difference and … survive.

Faith strode to Naina's workstation and announced gaily "I got the project! Paul has approved it. He overrode Surinder's directive! He also said that he would speak to Chanchal on Anita's rating and look into why I still hadn't been given a laptop. He himself brought the last point up again. I think he'll now dig up anything he has on Surinder along with these big ones. He's bringing Chanchal into this! Ain't that great?"

Naina was all ears. "Wow! Come on, come on. Spill the beans! Tell me everything, word to word." She urged Faith.

She relayed the entire conversation to Naina who couldn't have been more delighted. Surinder was fine with Naina but what she had heard had totally soured her towards him as well as Anita.

"Let's celebrate, Princess style! I know, we'll go to this cute place that I've always wanted to go for dinner" Faith wanted to rejoice at their mini- victory. At least, if nothing else, she got a project to work on.

They went to a posh, interesting little place, with the best live band in the city that does amazing everything! It was bang on the MG Road, adjacent to the Sahara Mall. Little did they know that this little dinner at "The Fox" would serve as initiation to a ritual of these closest of friends celebrating successes, drowning their sorrows, fighting over nothing, or ending it all!

✾✾✾

This was their first outing, faith and naina's. And it was something memories are made of.

Faith introduced Naina to wine. Naina teased Faith on why she always needed to be so "*Posh*". Naina wasn't much of a drinker and on occasions when she was, it was more Bacardi and Coke rather than wine or champagne.

They toasted

"Here's to woman power and the power of "right""

"Here's to small victories and gala dinners!"

"And to screwing Surinder royally"

They ordered more food than they could fathom. From "Djaj Makhloobar", an exotic rice and mutton dish from the Arab states to English style Fish and Chips, they experimented with all that sounded interested.

The band added another angle that would make it memorable for them. The lead singer, Kevin, was hot! They kidded each other about him and requested song after song till he took a break. They had another thing in common, music. They enjoyed the mushy ballads, the oldie Goldie romantics of "*our*" era viz. the 80s, soft rock, boy bands.

They talked about nothing in particular, just easy, comfortable to and fro-ing of banter. All in all, it was a contented hour that passed by too quickly and it was time to go back to work.

"Oops, more like three hours", Naina finally noticed our waiter hovering all by his lonesome near the bar. "The cleaners are out! Shit, we're the only ones in this restaurant. Where did the time fly by?"

Faith with three glasses of wine down was so merry, she wouldn't have noticed had they shut the lights off and locked the damn place up with them sitting right where they were.

"Nainz, I just don't feel like going back to work. And, we shouldn't with the alcohol we've consumed. Anyhow, work wise, we're pretty through for the day."

"Hey. You make me sound like a "run out of the town" supermarket. Nainz, no one's ever called me that before", Naina giggled. She was totally under the influence with close to two wine goblets down.

Faith laughed. "Yeh. That's cool, ain't it? You already got all this food inside of you. From all that we've eaten, I'm sure that pretty much covers all the major *and minor* food groups. You're set for life!"

"Shoot! Look what rubbish we're talking!" Now it was Faith's turn to giggle.

"Yeah, let's paint the town red!" said Naina with a naughty look in her eye.

Faith laughed, "My! My! Someone's in a vixy mood. I got a better suggestion. Let's go to my apartment. You've not seen it yet and I want to show you my place. It's very special to me. You should at least know see the hue and cry is about."

"Perfect ideaaa! Let's go"

"I can cook you a midnight snack", Faith kidded and got a severe reaction from both their stomachs. "Maybe not tonight. Huh?"

"Yeah but I'll take a rain check on that one"

When the bill came, both jumped up to flick it. Faith got to it first and would not hear of Naina paying or splitting. "Listen, going Dutch sucks! It doesn't matter who pays and today was totally my treat".

Meanwhile, Naina got another of her bright ideas. "You know what we should do? Keep the bill, split it in half and write something on it for keepsake. We won't show each other what we're writing till we're finished and then both of us can read it to each other"

"Cool one! Here you go. Do the deed."

When they shared notes, they were shocked! Barring the language, they wrote the same thing, in concept!

Naina wrote -

Faith…we finally go out for Dinner together! 'FOX' is an awesome place…

To our aspiring careers, Anita's downfall…and many more such dinners…

Here's to you and me… I love the taste of 'Wine'! That's the discovery of the day!!

… Luv Naina

Faith wrote -

2 'foxy' ladies…so cool, so bright, so smart!

*☺ Modesty aren't a virtue * winks *!*

Kick the buggers in the ass, let them rot, let them 'fraught' (Is this really a word??? ☺)

This is to 'us' and our war. To 'us', the blood sisters! … Faith

To date, it's always been this way.

✽✽✽

Naina was curious to see how people lived in complexes like "The Park". It had a reputation of being absolutely heavenly but she had never visited before. The security was so tight. It would be right to say that even a bird could not fly over if it did not have a residence inside.

When they entered, Naina was really in awe of the ambience of the place. Beautiful fountains marked the park boundaries and the central arcade. Palm trees, beautiful lilies and wild flowers grew in manicured lots. The lighting was subdued and extended a warm glow to everything. The glamorous residents were coming out of royal towers in their classy glitterati and waiting for their drivers to return with their equally royal cars to probably attend a formal dinner or function.

But, as they came to Faith's apartment, Naina noticed a lived-in, hominess to the house. Although, it was decorated elaborately, but there was nothing overwhelming about it. This house was a home.

Another surprise as she came through the long corridor marked with beautiful paintings and consoles, was finding Fuzzy relaxing on Faith's favorite chaise lounge. He was spread sideways, all fours out, and it was evident, he knew he was loved.

"Faith, I completely forgot to tell you before! I saw you the other day at the market where you found Fuzzy"

"Really?? You have some memory!"

"Well... It's strange that I did remember because ordinarily I have awesome observational skills ☺... I don't even remember what I wore yesterday... I am that bad! So normally, I wouldn't have noticed you at all but I did. Strange!! You know...first impressions. The first impression you create is a little... well, you know" Naina stalled trying to find the right words.

"Yes, yes! Do go on... I'm most intrigued." Faith egged her on 'cuz she was indeed interested to know. She liked to intimidate people with her presence because that meant that she had an element of control over them and that they would think twice before trying to take advantage of her. That dictated the way she dressed and how she carried herself.

'Well... you know, strong and over-powering...ready to claw. Someone, they can't take *pangas* with. 'The Touch me not ATTITUDE! But, when I saw you cradling Fuzzy, I happened to see some bit of the real you...its rare u know', Naina winked.

"You may not consider yourself as very observant but you are quite perceptive. I applaud you for that, *mon dieu*!" Faith cried out theatrically.

"But, I thank you for the compliment about the real me. That was nice. So, let's get some nice cool lemonade and chat then, shall we?"

"Haan Bhai! I m glad that we have such similar tastes. That's exactly what I want to do now too! And stop being so formal... No thank-youzzz between us" Naina ribbed Faith.

And then all night long they went back to when they were little. Like two teenage girls, they chatted about their heartaches, their dreams, giggled on silly jokes, cried over their failures, shared secrets, nothing too serious though. Tonight they would just live it up and leave their skeletons where they belong, in the past...

They had no idea though that their celebration would be short lived, that the war had only just begun

***

Next few days went by in a jiffy... Naina busy with her usual routine of day-to-day ops management and faith with getting to know the business and searching for improvement areas for her black belt project. She had already been told by paul that the project needed to be completed in six months...

Faith had just entered office one day when Naina came rushing towards her.

'Get up Faith', she tugged. 'Lets go and grab a cuppa coffee... I need to tell you something!'

'*Arre* gimme 5 minutes. At least let me login', Faith pleaded.

'*Ufff*! Tell me what will you do by just logging in? Leave these things for the Vintage club. They do all this stuff for their computer to record their 'In' time, just to prove that they keep those long hours at office...even if its just killing time over irrelevant things!

'Ok, *Chalo baba*', Faith gave in.

They sat facing each other, Faith with her favorite Cold coffee and Naina with her *Masala Chai.*

'I've just heard from sources that Edwin is going to be in India next week!', Naina said excitedly.

Edwin steel was the Operations Head for CMORT, US and their immediate Customer. He was their key man, responsible for all the Operation decisions pertaining to the relationship between US and India, Operations.

'Really? From where?' Faith questioned.

'From the US of course...where else silly? What's happened to you today? Did you have breakfast?' Naina teased Faith.

'No No, I meant from where did you get to know that he's coming', Faith immediately defended herself.

'Darling, the word is 'Arriving'. I am sure he's sensible enough not to 'come' in front of the entire office,' Naina winked.

'Ahhhhhhhhh! You're crazy!!' Faith moaned. Both of them giggled.

'On a serious note, you know what that means Faith?'

'Nope but I'm sure you'll tell me' snickered Faith

'*Arre*, it means that its something of utter importance that's on the cards that he's going to discuss by personally being here or else he would have just stated it in our of the calls with Surinder or Chanchal. Anita just told me, as per the Grapevine, that hez arriving here to sign off more business with us! Isn't that Gr8!'

'Wow!!! That's amazing *Yaar*! Will it also affect your process in a major way? Will the incomplete application forms also increase considerably?' Faith asked.

Naina nodded.

'True, it may not increase my span as it would for others who take care of the data entry but still…more business means more opportunities…maybe someday it'll benefit me too', Naina let out a deep sigh. She had already drifted off into a thinking mode.

'Hello Madam', Faith shook Naina. 'Come back to office. Stop dreaming about Edwin.' It was now Faith's turn to tease.

'He he he… now that you've mentioned Edwin, he's actually quite handsome!'

'Really?' Faith's eyes lit up.

'Yaaaaaa', Naina smiled. He's tall with a strong build, fair complexion with sharp features, deep brown eyes with a killer smile and above all he's SINGLE!'

'Hmmm! That poses some interesting thoughts in my mind' Faith smiled naughtily

'But he's just not your type. You like dark, short, bulky and bald men *na*? He's just not it,' Naina made a sad face and then giggled again.

They both laughed out…

It reminded them back of their respective school days... when any talk about a boy could trigger off a series of giggles amongst the girls...

Now nearly twelve years later, they were living it again... together. It was strange... in such a short time, a strong bond had been formed between them where they cared a lot for each other, could now say anything and everything to each other... without being judgmental or be judged.

Naina's mobile phone rang. It was Aman from the vintage group. Surinder had called in for a meeting with all his managers.

Naina and Faith gulped down the last remains of their drinks and ran up for the meeting.

Surinder was pacing up and down in the conference room. With all his team seated around the huge round table, he wanted to make sure that he covered everyone personally.

'So have all of you understood what I am saying ? ', he asked the group.

'Sure boss', Anita replied smiling coyly at Surinder. She never missed an opportunity to suck up to her boss. Naina and Faith stole a glance at each other.

'Great ! Paraphrase it for me', he told her.

"Edwin Steel is coming to India next Monday for an important but confidential meeting. We don't know much of details as yet, however looking at our past performance, we expect him to sign off some more processes with us ! This would mean an immediate ramp up and more span for most of us !'

Surinder blinked his eyes in affirmation.

'Also, Remember Guys... This is BIG stuff. I want all of you to go all the way to win over Edwin. This account can do wonders for a lot of careers here and I do not want any mix-ups or goof –ups. Got It ?', he again asked the group.

'Yes Surinder'. 'Sure Surinder'. 'Right Boss' ......the room was filled with

All the way meant out of the way for Surinder.

And so the team set out to welcome their *Firang* customer.

Bay were cleaned, Pin up boards were updated, manuals updated, unnecessary furniture was removed, all waste papers were shredded and so forth.

Finally the D-day arrived and so did Edwin.

Faith rushed to Naina who was working on her desk.

'Hey Nain', She shook Naina.' Is her here?'

'Ah-ho...Ja vekh leh', Naina spoke in Punjabi pointing towards Surinder's cabin. Faith did not understand Punjabi but being with Naina had its effects. She was now able to understand some words so had started relating to the language.

'Okie Dokie ...I'll see u later.'

Naina smiled to herself as soon as Faith walked off. She loved deliberately dropping some Punjabi words in between while interacting with Faith just to see her reaction and her struggle to cope up with it...

Faith rushed towards Anita's desk. Her desk was right in front of Surinder's cabin and had a clear view of whatever happened inside. Anita had chosen that seat deliberately for dual purposes. One, she could see all the activities happening inside Surinder's cabin. She would then put two and two together to create a story and pass it on as Grapevine on the floor. She prided herself in being up to date with the latest news on the floor and the first one to know it!

And the other reason was that in between, she could also exchange some glimpses of Surinder...She had a huge crush on him and it was increasing with time.

"Oh God !', Naina though. "What a taste Anita has got. The famous saying that Beauty lies in the eyes of the beholder is absolutely true in her case. *Varna* Surinder ?", she smiled to herself.

Faith walked up to Anita and deliberately started a conversation with her. It was quite easy to do this with Anita. She loved chatting and could go on and on for hours at a stretch. In between she glanced at Surinder's cabin. And there he was with his back toward the door.

Faith tried to get a glimpse of Edwin from several angles but with no success. 'Turn *baba*...I wanna see you', she murmured. However all that she could get to see was his back.

He was just not turning around !

'Shit', Faith said out aloud and immediately regretted it.

'What?', questioned Anita who jerked out of her monologue by Faith's comment. She glanced surprisingly at Faith. 'Did I say something wrong?', she asked.

'Na...I was just thinking of the process load today. Naina is going to have a tough time managing the volumes.', Faith changed the topic immediately.

'Ah Yes ! That she will. But you know what, Naina's an amazing manager. She's handled it all before', Anita replied convincingly.

Even though they were competitors, Anita admired Naina for her work as did everyone else in the organization. Handling tough situations was Naina's strength. She did it with such ease that it appeared simple and easy. All her peers were curious to know her trade secret !

Faith's mind was still on Edwin. She had suddenly developed an urgency to see him though she couldn't figure out why.

She bid goodbye to Anita and walked back to Naina's desk.

Naina was in deep conversation with Bharat who was one of her Team leads. She saw Faith approaching her and gestured her to wait for five minutes.

The volumes were surging and it was a concerned Bharat who had approached Naina.

It was the 1st day of the month. The salaries had come in the bank accounts of the employees a day earlier so some associates who wanted to quit the job did so as they were just waiting for their salaries before resigning. Now Naina's team had 3 hits by a competitor who had just entered the market.

'Don't panic Bharat. 'Just go and use the cross trained pool of resources from our other processes to pitch in. Let me also speak to the managers of some other shops to provide some resources to help out.' Don't worry. We'll manage buddy', she smiled to put him at ease.

Bharat smiled back. He knew that she had a solution for everything. No matter how tough a situation was, Naina was always calm and composed and 'In control' for her team.

That's why she was nicknamed – *Sankat Mochan*' by her team members.

'*Sankat*' meant Danger and '*Mochan*' meant Remover.

In Hindu mythology, *Hanuman* was referred to as *Sankat Mochan.* He was the person who had a solution for everything and he helped *Lord Rama* out of trouble every time.

Naina Chopra was the *Hanuman* of CMort...the Danger remover or in other words the Solution provider for the process and her team respected her a lot for it !

Naina called her peers in other businesses for resource support who agreed to provide help. She updated Bharat on this and then gave some more instructions to him to supervise the queue. He then walked off assured. She took a deep breath and then waved to Faith to come over.

'Yes ma'am, had your fill?', she teased Faith.

'No *Yaar*', I couldn't see him. The Idiot had his back to me all this while', Faith complained.

'Sooooo Sad na', she teased again. 'Don't worry, you'll get to meet him soon', she reassured Faith.

'*Chal*, I've got to get on a Conference Call with Pam. I'll catch you later', Naina walked off.

PART FOUR

S… STEEL

Edwin truly had a way about him. He was young, way too young to be handling the portfolio that he was for CMort, US. He also had a huge potential to grow within the company. Pamela Watson a.k.a Pam was extremely fond of Edwin and not all of it was due to his drop dead gorgeous looks and oozing charm.

Naina was on the Transition committee along with Surinder and Anita for CMort. It was a golden opportunity for her to increase her visibility in the organization. She was running a successful process and her opinion was valued in the organization. The leadership had chosen her to work closely with Edwin to ensure a smooth Ramp-up that was expected to happen.

Earlier when she had been introduced to Edwin, her mind has instantly gone toward Faith. "He is gorgeous!" thought Naina. "And also the perfect distraction for Faith! I'm sure this guy could bring her out of this drought in her life. All Faith really needs is a good lay!"

As Edwin had greeted all of them one by one, Naina almost swooned at his deep voice.

"Naina. That's an amazing name. And how fitting it is! It's great to finally tie the voice to the face. Pleased to meet you", he smiled warmly as he shook hands with her.

'The pleasure is certainly mine', Naina grinned as she shook hands with him.

Surinder had instructed Naina to spend time with Edwin to update him of the process and showcase all the process improvements that had been made by her Team.

Through the next few days, they spend a lot of time together discussing the Global Business Delivery Model that was topping Edwin's agenda. In between she showcased the amazing work that she had done for the process. They had digitized a lot of trackers which had reduced Touch time for the loan applications. It was a team effort and she gave all the credit to her team for it. She also got him oriented to the facilities as this was his first visit to town; Surinder also presented the business metric dashboards and the numbers looked absolutely fine! Edwin displayed his pleasure in the business review and requested that he have one-on-one meetings with all the operations managers.

'I'll take care of it', Naina took the responsibility of his meeting with the operations managers.

'Hey Faith…Howz it going *Yaar*. We haven't been able to catch up in ages !', Naina spoke over the phone. She and Faith had not been able to spend time with each other for the past few days.

'Crazy Nain ! My project is killing me !', Faith moaned.

'I can bet that mine is crazier', Naina Sighed. 'Mr. Steel is taking a lot of my time and energy and I have not got any breather at all'

'I know, I heard he's tough', Faith stated.

'Yeah..that he is', Naina confirmed. 'But its good that he's here...from a relationship building perspective, it'll help us a lot.'

They kept chatting for a long time till one of them yawned and the other followed.

Promising to meet up with each other the next day, they signed off.

❦❦❦

Edwin was a coffee freak and insisted on taking Naina to Barista for his one on one. Naina was a tea addict and was more than glad to grab a hot cup. She readily accepted his invitation.

As they were walking to the elevators to go down to the ground level, Naina saw Faith flitting about in the adjacent bay.

Naina had raved the previous day to Faith about Edwin. Faith had portrayed immense excitement but she had not been able to fool Naina. Naina knew that Faith was masking that girly anticipation and wanting to meet the gorgeous new hunk in town. She also realized that it would not be easy to entice Faith on to Edwin and she had no idea whether Edwin would be interested at all. "But then if Edwin can't get Faith going then she might as well join the nunnery!"

A brilliant idea hit Naina as the lift opened at their floor. "Edwin, in the review yesterday, you have complimented Surinder on the presentation. I was wondering if you'd like to meet the person who envisaged that pitch?"

Edwin was definitely curious, as he had assumed that Surinder had done the handy work himself. "Sure. Why not !"

Faith was halfway through a complex multiple regression exercise for her project when Naina called out to her. "In a minute! I'll lose my train of thought, sweetheart"

Naina was nonplussed at the response, as was Edwin, she was sure! She caught a quick glance in his direction and was surprised to see him smiling at that. She cleared her throat and moved closer to Faith to get her attention once again. "Faith, I have someone I want to introduce you to."

Faith continued to sit but turned round on her chair. As she looked up, Edwin made for a great sight but not what she had anticipated.

'Edwin, meet Faith. She's the official presentation maker for us', Naina smiled naughtily.

'Hello Faith, how are you doing today', Edwin extended his hand.

"Oh, good afternoon! Pleased to meet you, Edwin."

"Pleasure, I'm sure! I came here to congratulate on your great work for the review yesterday"

Faith accepted his compliment and extended her own for the work she's heard he has done for their business.

Naina stood there, rooted, as the conversation between Faith and Edwin eased on. Neither was willing to end it and move on to their business. Faith had forgotten her analysis as Edwin had his schedule. They talked of how the review went, when Faith had joined and what she felt about what she had seen of the processes so far. Edwin shared his experiences with CMort and Faith shared her initial frank opinions about the changes that ought to be invested into.

Finally, Naina interrupted their dialogue, "Edwin, we should probably get to that coffee you promised me else Surinder will take my case for delaying you."

"Oh, yes! They are keeping me on a tight leash around here" Edwin apologized to Faith, politely, for having to go.

"As can be expected" Faith replied, winking to Naina.

"Please carry on with your meeting. It was nice meeting you", continued Faith.

"Likewise and let's see if I can clear my schedule to review your project as well"

"That'll be great. I need all the support I can muster. Thanks."

As Edwin moved away, he felt an urgent need to look back at Faith. Faith had seated herself but continued to look in his direction. What he did next shocked both Faith as well as Naina but, most of all, him; he waved at Faith. Faith waved back with a grin.

✾✾✾

As Edwin whisked through meetings that day, his mind kept wandering to Faith. In that short span, she had made quite a dent of an opinion on him.

"She looks so bright and classy yet so deliciously sexy!" thought Edwin just as Chanchal enquired something of him. "I beg your pardon? I didn't quite catch that."

"Shucks! Focus on the meeting, maestro!" Edwin prodded himself as Chanchal repeated his question.

Later that evening, Surinder had planned a dinner for Edwin with the entire managerial team of CMort.

Park Baluchi was a hot spot. Located in the prime central market area of Gurgaon, it was a favorite hangout for food lovers. On Friday nights, it was packed with people and the group had to wait for nearly twenty minutes before they could finally get a table.

Meanwhile, they had ordered starters and soon their table was filled with platters of assorted kebabs.

As they nibbled at the food, someone suggested wine. 'That's a good idea', added Preeti who was the training manager. 'Wine for everyone', Surinder ordered.

'Not for me. I've got to go back to work', Naina replied.' By the way Preeti, what happened to the ladies night out that you were planning?'

"*Aare Yaar*, I want to do it but *kya karen*, time is a constraint and it keeps getting delayed… Lets do something next week. We women, too, have a right to enjoy ourselves.

What say, team?', she asked to no one in particular. No one answered back either. This was quite normal with Preeti. People had shorter than normal attention spans with her. This seemed to be the story of her life. Apparently, this was true also for her estranged husband, especially in their "*alone*" times.

The dinner was fun with little office talk. People generally stayed away from the Big Celebration Topic though. Surinder, however, felt it prudent to toast to Edwin and his brilliant support of Stan Inc.

Edwin smiled his charismatic yet modest smile as Surinder rendered his toast.

"What an ass!" he thought. He had a considerably terrible opinion of the way Surinder ran his business. He had seen CMort operations at Stan Inc. being run down to tatters under Surinder's leadership. Apart from this, he could not understand why the CMort leadership would want to outsource their business when they could do a better job themselves. Underwriting was one of their most critical processes… and the financial penalties, if anything were to seriously go wrong…

Edwin tore himself from his reverie to the task at hand. He had to convince Surinder to let him study the India operations in depth. He had already laid down the foundation in that he would want to grow their operations in India and Stan Inc. was the most obvious choice for the amazing performance they had displayed over the years.

"I am personally disgusted just to think it but I had to give Surinder that ray of hope for him to give me what I need to get my business back!" thought Edwin.

As he turned his attention back to Surinder, his eyes stopped at Faith. She was immersed in a deep conversation with Naina. Suddenly, something that Naina said seemed to amuse her and she laughed out aloud. In all the chitter chatter, that melodious laugh fell like music on Edwin's ears. In the last few days, Edwin could not remember ever seeing Faith smile. It was a beautiful smile that mesmerized him.

A couple of days earlier during one of their coffee chats, Naina had told him about her friendship with Faith...that they were best friends. She had mentioned how they'd met and he had had a hearty laughter at their expense at that incident !

He look at both of them again.

One look at them both together had said it all. Of what was between them. It was surprising to him as well as to how could two girls so different from each other, almost in every manner, be so close. They certainly had a strong chemistry between them even though they were so chilled about it.

Naina with the most beautiful eyes that he'd ever seen and a glowing face that spelled so much warmth was the livelier of the two. Her eyes shone every time she spoke about the passion she had for her work. He'd seen that himself when she interacted with her team and was impressed by her amazing people handling skills. Not to mention, her strong Operations background which clearly showed in her performance. Faith on thc other hand was simply sexy…too sexy in every way ! He was instantly attracted to her. She had this mysterious look about her which was drawing him towards her.

This had never happened to him before. He was one who did not believe in love let alone love at first sight! He had for the last 5 years lived a bachelors' life and his parents had lost hope of his ever marrying.

"Oh, hell! Why the f*** am I thinking of marriage, of all things! Hey dude, concentrate on the mission at hand."

"Surinder, I would like to spend the next 2 days on the floor studying how your guys work these processes. Do you think we can reschedule my meetings on the calendar you created for my visit so that I can do that?"

"OK. But may I ask why you feel the need to do this? After all, you said yourself that you are very happy with the numbers we presented to you."

"Oh yes, that I am. In fact, it is because of your fabulous performance that I want to learn how you manage such effective operations. I want to share these best practices with Pam and leverage these learnings to better our operations back home."

"Oh! Pam? Why, that will be great! Sure, I will share your modified calendar with you tomorrow morning."

"One more thing, two lead underwriters from my team in the US are due to fly in tomorrow. I wanted your team leads to meet with them and interact. They can learn a lot from them as these guys have been doing this for over a decade. Anyhow, if they could also spend the next couple of days with your teams, that would help our case further. If you know what I mean."

"Sure, Edwin. I'll have the managers arrange that."

"So simple!" thought Edwin. This was his chance to prove to his boss, Pam, that the grass root operations for this business was indeed in the gutter, as he had known all along. His lead underwriters would cover all front line operations and employee satisfaction in his investigation and he would delve deeper into the MIS reports.

With that, he again focused his attention on the other end of the table at Faith. She seemed pre-occupied and pensive, as she read something from her mobile. He wondered what it could be. She aroused his curiosity and he desperately wanted to solve this mystery. Alas! He was here for just another week.

He would have to schedule that project review meeting in order to speak to her in private. And fast…

✾✾✾

When we're kids our parents teach us stuff like not to swear nor be rude to others, to be considerate of other's feelings, to always be sincere and truthful and so on.

All good! Faith thought. But as we grow up, most of us unlearn these because of incidents that make us. She wondered if her parents had worked on her in vain. Perhaps. Maybe not, on second thought. There still was some good left.

But would she then not teach her own kids these simple rules of good behavior? Of course, she would. That's really a moot point. But, why would she, she questioned? Why, if their entire lives they need to work on undoing that learning and feeling guilty about it on top of it? Like any good mother, she did not want to lade her children with guilt of any sort. But, she still would.

She pondered on this vague idea a bit and then she came up with an answer. She would teach them in the hope that they do not go through the kind of things people, who forget these golden rules, go through.

Faith was a thinker and when she got tired, her mind still kept working and thinking ridiculously silly thoughts like these. Post mortem, Faith muttered, after quite some time had passed, "Pish Tosh, Faith! All this rubbish does not make sense! Where does your mind keep wandering, pray tell?" She chided herself. But her mind did not respond, it did not feel the need. It had a mind of its own.

It went on another tangent and as she was thinking about the five pounds that she would *lurve* to lose and how she would hate to go on a diet and not get to splurge on her daily dose on cheese toasts, melted chocolate pastries and Lays American Cheese and Onion wafers. Just as she had mentally finished devouring the "fast foods" segment and moving on to Dal Makhani, Pathar kebab, and butter naans, her reverie was interrupted by a call on her mobile.

She had not eaten well at the dinner just because she had made up her mind that she would not condone any celebration that Surinder was initiating even if the company was paying for it! Now, she was starving and the thought of all that food did not help. She answered the call a little irritated at her for being so stuck-up, "Yeah".

"It's me. I have to tell you something urgently."

"*Kya Hua*, tell me", Faith sensed the urgency in Naina's voice.

"I went home with Anita in the same cab tonight. She has probably not realized how close we've become in this short while. She, therefore, tried to sell me a lot of bullshit about you."

"What the hell? What kind of stuff?" Faith had a short fuse when it came to misunderstandings and people deliberately lying and conniving to create them.

"We need to talk on this at length. It'll have its ramifications for sure. It's time for damage control… if we can at all. Let's first analyze the root causes for why she would have said what she did to me and what she wanted to achieve",Naina was obviously worried.

Faith thought that Naina was looking at this like a business related problem. It was an interesting observation because when people work in this industry or any industry for too long, their personal lives become an extension of their work. The lingo they use or their outlook changes to reflect that they have in the office.

"Yes, well… I can't wait till later. Let's discuss this over the phone. Tell me exactly what she told you"

Naina, being she, carried on for the next half an hour on all that Anita had said. The gist of it was that Anita had deducted from their discussion about Rohan and Faith's stay with his family in London that she had gone all the way with him before marriage, that they stayed in the same room, same house for months together and then the engagement broke off.

She then went on to tell Naina that she ought to be careful of her because Faith was certainly promiscuous and could, and would, go to any lengths in order to succeed. In the interim, Naina would lose out because she would find herself in the middle of the two camps; one being the conscientious and the righteous who do good work and go home and the other who have all the "connections" and succeed even more than the former. Anita feigned concern for Naina to warn her that she did not want Camp One to disown her because of her association with someone like Faith.

Neither Naina nor Anita knew at the moment that Faith had actually been married to Rohan during that period. That was a little piece of personal information she had kept to herself.

But she planned to tell Naina soon about Rohan. She made a mental note of it.

"Thank God, for small mercies! God knows what these people would've started on had I been open about that!" Faith counted her blessings in this tiring tirade of predicaments.

Nonetheless, Faith was livid and fuming by the time Naina finished.

***

Faith wanted to take the bull by its horns and rock it's world and not in a nice way either.

Faith walked to her desktop and decided to distract herself with the e-mail for the day. She had already decided after what Naina had told her last night that she would ensure that Anita's project went backwards rather than vice versa whilst Naina would soon complete hers and celebrate her Green Belt Quality certification, much to Anita's greatest dismay.

A Green Belt certification is a step before a Black Belt certification. It is highly prestigious and a great career booster and Naina deserved it with her fabulous project.

As she sifted through organization's junk mail, she came across a meeting request from Edwin for the project review for later that day. She accepted it but stopped to wonder how he had managed to move his meetings and reschedule so promptly to make time for her. And more importantly, why?

Yesterday, when she had met Edwin for the first time, she had definitely felt a spark. He was strikingly attractive! And important too. She could really do with an ally... Edwin could prove to be a great resource and hopefully a friend. She had liked him instantaneously and could identify with his thoughts about running the business.

"Hello there, Faith!"

Faith jerked at the sudden disruption in her mental trance. "Hey! I'm really sorry for startling you. I didn't realize that you were so lost in thought."

Faith turned around to feast her eyes on Edwin. "Edwin! Oh, don't worry about it. So, what brings you to my part of the town?"

"Well, I had a half hour or so before my next meeting with Paul and thought I'd pick your brains to really understand what his reasons could be in wanting to meet with me. I'll be honest with you. I've been thinking about our first interaction yesterday and I see you as an intelligent woman who speaks her mind and opinions openly. So, what gives?"

Faith was taken aback at his honest confession of his assessment of her. But, she had to give him his intuitive abilities! And she began to tell Edwin about how Paul and Surinder were competing for the next level, a position that was reserved for only one of the two. Chanchal would favor the person who, according to him, deserved it the most.

For Surinder, a clear win would be to get more business from Edwin. And Paul wanted a foot in the door with him as well as CMort was a volatile business where the Quality function could really make a difference.

Edwin shared his own thoughts about the way Surinder had run the India operations of CMort down.

As both, Faith as well as Edwin, stopped for a breather, they shared a strange look. They were equally astounded by the amount they had shared with the other and that in the bargain of exchanging views they had come to exchange much more!

She had no idea though that Edwin, in spite of his fondness for Faith, was making pointers for the easiest win of his career!

✾✾✾

The next month went by in a flurry. Faith had finally done her training and was on top of things. Her own project was running as smoothly as circumstances afforded. She had gotten into the groove and used to the reckless and unprofessional handling between the managers, the unrelenting pursuit of the pot of gold under the rainbow, far away into the horizon.

But one day the game changed… for the worse, of course.

Traipsing through an exceptionally tough day, Faith decided on a coffee. Faith was lost in thought on an especially troubling problem she was currently working on. Each chilled burst of life seemed to fizzle into the fuddled moment until a man at her cafeteria table distracted her attention to his raspy clearing of the throat.

"Hi Faith. Remember me?" said he when she finally looked up from her abstraction.

Faith hated when people asked her that and she hoped he didn't go on to ask her his name. Some people do that. They say, "Hi *Beta. Aapko hamari yaad hai? Batao mera naam kya hai?*"

And Faith who is terrible at remembering names would go in her equally terrible Hindi accent. "But, of course *uncle-ji! Aap kya kehte ho. Hum aapko bhi kabhi bhool sakte hain. Aapne to hume naaraz kar diya*" and that would silence most men into blushing and playfully pretending to dowse Faith's, just as pretentious, tantrum. That teasing to and fro-ing would go on for time enough for the old bugger to forget where it had all begun. At that cue, Faith would beg her courteous departure from the conversation and move on.

In contrast to her photographic visual memory, that for names and numbers was atrocious.

Coming back, Faith tried to focus furiously on trying to place the face before her. That guy with the sissy yellow shirt with the mucky collar in the meeting with the higher ups last week? Or the one who flung his fork, high up in the air, at the formal do, in one of his animated reviews of his recent winning trip to the client site only to land, circumspect, into the Chairman's wine glass with a "Career limiting" splash? Can't be. He'd be a gonner by now. Hey! He's the one from the 2nd week Black belt training. He kept fooling around the entire week. Finding lewd associations to statistical terminologies like *inflection point* or *delta*. Shucks! What A LOSER! When was that? 2 weeks back? Hell! I'll never remember his name. But, here goes again…

"Hey there! Of course, I do. So, how're you and the bigwig?"

"Oh! I'm no one important. Just the ordinary monk who got the best job in the best company of the best country of the world!" And he laughed.

Man! Is he weird or what? Thought she! Is no one normal in this world anymore? That was totally a rhetorical. She knew the answer already. The delusional Miss Know It All.

"So, then. How've you been? The whole building's buzzing about you nowadays. The hot new black belt on Floor 2! No wonder everyone's calendars show a new high on the time spent on "waiting at the elevators for a lift to come by"

Faith laughed at the seams with no hint of the "eye". "I wish it were so. At least that way some thing would've gone my way"

"Hey! Let's go for dinner soon." While his hand came to rest, a little too suggestively, at Faith's left shoulder blade.

Faith was taken aback but rose to the occasion promptly. Shrugging her shoulders so that his hand slipped off 'em "Aren't you too married to be taking, to dinner, a single girl like me?"

"Hey! I would say I've been married enough to be taking out a *girl like you*"

At that insinuation, Faith lost it. "What the hell do you mean by that?"

"Well… don't act so shocked. Word does get around, after all, I am powerful within the company and I can really get you places. If YOU oblige that is. And isn't this what you really want too? I know, you know, that you do and you know what, I do too!" His smile was mocking and menacing at the same time.

Faith was disgusted to the core. The coffee was beginning to threaten its way up and she did not want to look weak in front of this fucked up asshole.

Faith would've liked to tell him to go fuck himself to power-play kingdom but she let her actions do it for her. She looked him straight in the eyes, brought her hand up to his face level. He suddenly realized she would strike him and he staggered a step back.

He was stunned to see what happened next. He looked at it in complete shock. In the middle of the cafeteria, Faith had up, in plain view for all to see and directly in front of the senior AVPs face, her middle finger.

They stood like that for what seemed like an eternity, to both, when Faith winked at him, turned on her heels and walked off.

Faith's integrity and reputation had been attacked. Naina and she knew who were behind it. They also knew they could not let it go easy.

✤✤✤

Sometimes, there are such forces at work that there is little one can do to avert ill wills. Whether these forces are against you or for you, we cannot say for sure. There is a dichotomy here because whether all the bad stuff is really bad for us or just happens so that we may learn from it and become stronger is a mystery.

Some maintain that pain is pain and whilst a whole load of learning happens, sure it does, but it would be folly to go looking for trouble just to become more enlightened.

Others believe that before we set out on our lives, we create a journey for ourselves, our lives' path that has its roadblocks, hurdles, joys and heartaches tuned to our own personal needs. It is all put together for us, by us.

What is déjà vu? They say that when we go through an experience and suddenly get this strong feeling that this has happened before, well, it's nothing but a faint retained memory over lifetimes, before the current lifetime, *when one was creating one's own destiny.*

Faith found place in the second category of theorists. She believed that there are strong higher forces that guide us through our lives but we actually create our own destinies and fate is really not an ill word, it is we.

Naina too partnered her in this belief.

Faith had introduced her to the Brian Weiss world by gifting her 'Only Love is Real' and she had real all his books then, one after another. This book had brought peace in her life that she was searching so desperately. Peace about what life is, of why people are what they are and most importantly why things happen, the way they do.

She had learnt that people meet because they are meant to learn from each other…specially from each other's experiences as well as their own and depart once the learning is complete. This hold good for life too. Once a learning is complete, people move on. She finally understood that not all relationships are meant forever. All that we can do is live'em and learn from them.

She had gone through a lot of pain in her life and the past still hounded her. This philosophy had helped her ease it.

She recognized still that there are forces larger than you because that's what happens when fates of multiple beings entwine. Right now, she felt that either she had planned a long, hard ride for herself or her destiny was playing hardball with others'.

Albeit all the hard work and long hours, playing on Paul, Faith could not douse the fire that Surinder and Anita had spread. The spirit of a grapevine is such that even the Gods can just about drink wine off it!

Faith, being the eternal optimist, adopted another approach to handling this: Ignorance.

She focused on what had become really important to her, her work, attaining knowledge and, most of all, her friendship with Naina: the bane of her sanity.

Positive forces are so much more powerful than the negative. This has been proved time and again, in Epics, in movies, literature and, above all, theatre (even though the good guys ordinarily die in the end, it just shows the intensity of the emotions and becomes the driving force for the maniacal addiction to that form of art. Even in death, they win!).

What Faith and Naina could not achieve by playing the game by their oppositions' rules, they did by the power of friendship. They became such a force to reckon with that nothing could touch them, break their trust in the other, and their relationship, that people forgot about Faith and her past or present occupations. They obsessed over how could this so-called friendship be real?

Most of them waited for time to reveal who was *using* whom. Certainly, Faith was because she was the cunning one, wasn't she? But, Naina finally completed her project, didn't she? All 'cuz of Faith helping her out? They gambled on it for time, for the victim and the offender.

Four months had passed since their first meeting and they saw a bud bloom into a flower. Yuck! Such a clichéd phrase. But it was just like that. Not that they didn't have their set of problems or fights.

PART FIVE

THE COUNTDOWN BEGINS

FINDING THE WITNESS

Faith Jones closed her eyes in thoughtful silence. She always found the twilight hours relaxing and perfect for practicing her newfound love: Meditation.

Today, however, Faith was restless and slightly annoyed at her lack of concentration. Her mind kept drifting off to her infuriating colleagues at work, her hair styling appointment the day after, her dog that would need to be walked soon, her past, her life… everything except for the task at hand. "Focus, Faith! You can do this", she muttered and readied herself once again.

Modern physiology, scientific research, says that between the two eyebrows is the gland, which is the most mysterious part in the body. This gland, called the pineal gland, is the third eye of the Tibetans – *Shivanetra:* the eye of Shiva, of tantra. Between the two eyes there is a third eye existing but ordinarily it is non-functioning. You have to do something about it to open it. It is not blind. It is simply closed. When you attain complete focus at the third eye, suddenly you become a witness. Through the third eye, you can see thoughts running like clouds in the sky or people moving on the street. You become an observer and, sometimes, you become the very essence of breath, *prana.* In this, you become clairvoyant!

Faith had become enchanted with this technique when she had heard of it. After having practiced it for months, she had attained some measure of success and had become more content and at peace, as an individual. "Attention between the eyebrows, let the mind be before thought" Faith pressed on. Her breathing became deeper and her body felt lighter.

Faith realized that she had a lot going for her. She hailed from a well-known family in the metropolis. She was an extremely attractive brunette, tall with a fabulous figure to match, 28 and very attached. She was also very aware of the fact that she, Faith Jones, was a catch!

"Become a witness... simply observe all thoughts that enter your mind. Keep the focus..." Faith's eyelids fluttered. Her mind was now completely coordinated with her breathing. "Breathe in... Follow the path that the fresh oxygen takes through your body... Slowly, breathe out".

For the first time, Faith began to see vibrant images through her mind's eye. "Such bright colors!" she thought. They were so vivid that she physically felt her eyes smart. Faith knew that she was coming to experience a strange phenomenon.

Suddenly, she saw images that realized her worst nightmare and she was shocked! She gasped for air and jumped out of her stance, violently! Although, she was now out of her meditative state, she realized that she was shivering and had broken out in a cold sweat. "That was completely surreal!" Faith said abashed.

Faith justified this as just another experience towards cleansing her mind off the recent events in her life. Her joining a leading Business Process Outsourcing company, Stan Inc., as a Quality Manager had opened her eyes to corporate political dominion in a new *vistar*. The BPO industry has it's own dynamics as did Stan Inc. The industry is fairly young of just about 10 years. The people who joined this industry as young college graduates are now 30 odd year olds and leading large divisions at extremely high positions, and even higher salaries. Needless to say, this kind of power, and resources, goes to their heads and modesty becomes a rare find. The workplace becomes their playground and politicking their forte.

Faith also, however, saw the benefits that this industry had bestowed on the Indian economy, the growing purchasing power, the exponentially growing employment opportunities, the excellent work ethics, for the most part. She had, in such a short time, developed an unbridled passion for this company and the young people who worked for her processes. They had so much energy and commitment for those just out of college and starting their careers.

She had also found love. Much to her complete surprise and amazement, she had found love in their dynamic, gorgeous hunk of a client. He had whisked her off her feet on their first meeting and it had been a roller coaster ride ever since. Edwin, of part Indian-part Mexican origin; Edwin, of late night calls and beautiful dreams; Edwin, of sweetness and brilliance; Edwin, who could do no wrong!

She dragged herself to the kitchen, opened the refrigerator door and picked out her favorite mineral water bottle. She gulped down half the contents in one draw and balanced her delicate frame on the counter. She was now feeling a little more human and she let down a sigh of relief convincing her that this was just her mind playing games. She, then, trampled to the adjoining dining room and decided she would watch a spot of television.

Faith realized that she had an addiction. To her, watching television, incessantly, was a necessary modern evil. She flicked the channels and landed on the news. "How boring! Nothing but murder, molestation, theft, corruption. Blah!"

Faith raised her arm to move on to her favorite channel when she stopped short. Her eyes fell on her mobile and she saw a blinker for an unread message from her supervisor, Surinder Singh. As she read it, her mouth fell open with shock, her throat constricted with fear, and a chill ran up her spine.

Faith felt her anger rising giving way to helplessness as she looked on.

The message read, "All Hands on Deck. Edwin is stopping the current ramp-up of 100 underwriters"

Her worst nightmare had, indeed, come true!

Her life had again come full circle. With promises of more business, that Edwin had never intended to keep, he had put at risk the careers of the 100 people hired for the business? How would Faith save grace? And how could Faith let another man betray her again?

THE SILVER LINING

It took 20 seconds for Faith's life to go from near perfect to disastrous. Her business, her people, and her heart... everything was on the line. Edwin? How could he do this? And she had bared everything to him. Everything? And to what detriment? She would have to speak to Surinder to really know what is happening.

She ran to get dressed. In 10 minutes, she was driving to work. On the way, she called Naina.

"Oh honey! I can't believe Surinder's message! And Edwin? Why would he do this? He was so pleased when he left. What could have happened in the last month? Did you guys fight or something?" Naina was close to delirium.

"Babe. Calm yourself. I'm in a goddamn crazy movie right now. I can't believe it either. And NO, we did not fight or something! What would that have to do with this?"

"Ok. Ok baba! Where are you? I'm in the cab right now about a half an hour away."

"I've left home and will reach in 10 or so. I'll see you there then."

"Alright and listen don't get worried. I don't think he would try to hurt you. I saw how much he cares for you when we met over that dinner, just before he left for the U.S. And god knows, you both have only got stronger over the last month."

"Or so I thought. Anyways, let's hear what Surinder has to say and then I'll talk to Edwin. I need to get in touch with him soon… else I'll go mad thinking about this."

"Yeah, do that. Take care now… I'll catch you soon."

"Cya Nain."

The conversation had got Faith to the point of crazydom. Her mind and past experiences were playing games with her and she kept conjuring wild stories. Was Edwin using her to get the information he could not discover from others? Was there someone in the US who was forcing him to stop the ramp-up? Had he wanted to do this all along? Did he find something that prompted him to? But then why did he not confide in her…

As she reached the office building, she flung her long legs from her car and made a dash for it.

Her relationship with Edwin had developed overnight. After that short conversation, Edwin had gone on to meet Paul and had definitely found him to be the lesser of the two evils. He had shared that with Faith in their project review. The review had lasted precisely 10 minutes out of the one-hour he had booked with her. He had genuinely appreciated her good work in spite of no formal quality training. There were insights that Faith had drawn her work upon that even Edwin had been pleasantly surprised with. He had lent her his full support and, to toast that, he had invited her to dine with him that evening.

"Can I have the pleasure of your company for dinner tonight?" he had enquired with a half-cocked smile and soft eyes that bore into her like a butter knife.

"You may but only if you would let me do the cooking for us. You deserve some home cooked food. What say?"

"It's an offer I can not refuse, m'lady. I am dying for some good ol' Indian home food!"

✱✱✱

"Faith! Over here, in Venus." Aman called out to her. Venus was the name of one of the larger meeting rooms in the building. This was also where most of the conference calls took place, except for the boardroom.

Faith almost half-ran to the room which she saw was already half-full with the other managers and Surinder. Paul had also made an appearance. Judging by the speed, at which the others had appeared to work on a Saturday, Faith knew that Surinder had delayed sending her that message till much later. But, this was not the time to get sidetracked by frivolity.

Faith entered and sat near the exit door. The room was extremely pensive as folks waited for everyone to join them. As Naina entered the room, she joined Faith.

"Have they begun?"

"No. But I presume we will soon that almost everyone's here."

Surinder cleared his throat to get everyone's attention. "All of you know that the news that I am to share does not bode good tidings. I wrote to you all saying that Edwin is pulling CMort back from Stan Inc. It is true, indeed."

Faith's heart sank once again as she heard Surinder say those words. Instantly she felt Naina's hand on hers. She looked at Naina and their eyes met.

'I am with you' was written all over Naina's.

Surinder continued to explain, "When Edwin visited India he raved about building a beautiful partnership with the

India team. However, the true purpose of his visit was not to outsource more business but to prevent the current ramp-up of 100 from occurring. As his span of control was being reduced in the US by adding more people in India, he was internally displeased. His team of subject matter experts, the lead underwriters that covered his visit, donned the cover of studying best practices with the hope of unraveling some dirt on the process. And they did, enough for Edwin to return to the US and create the worst image of Indian operations management with Pam. He even provided documented proofs of the mistakes that have been allegedly made by the Indian team, and have never been looked at or corrected, subsequently. I still do not believe that all of that evidence was real but the indications were clear enough for Pam to evaluate our relationship with CMort."

Paul felt the need to interject and draw Surinder's point to conclusion "We had a call with Pam yesterday. She told us in certain words that there was no way that they were going to siphon off more business to Stan Inc."

Surinder stopped to look at the solemn faces around the room. Faith was on her seat's edge waiting for the meeting to be over so she could speak to Edwin and get his perspective out. There was no way he could have been so manipulative and, for what, to stop a ramp-up from occurring? What difference would 100 team members make to his span and power game?

Surinder continued, "This is not all. We did not want to divulge this information via SMS but we must now. Pam was furious with Edwin's findings and the state of current affairs. She clearly laid down the rules for us: They want to not only stop any future ramp-ups but pull back the entire business! All of 800 people!"

There were a series of loud gasps as Surinder finished the last sentence. No one knew how to react and there was uproar across the room.

Naina and Faith exchanged horrified looks. In a moment, Naina's life flashed. The last four months had taken over her being, for good and for bad. All their jobs and careers were at stake. 800 + careers on the line! She thought Edwin had been a blessing in disguise for the business and for her best friend but life had only been playing tricks with them, once again.

"Guys! Guys, please listen up. There is a silver lining… a thin one but there is a way out of this situation." Surinder got everyone's morbid attention. He continued "Pam has laid down the law: Re-engineer the business or they would take it back, all if it in 2 months!"

PART SIX

FRIENDS "FORWARD"?

Chapter 1
THE CONTENDER

DAY 2

Naina was in one of her exceptionally dreary moods today. She had dragged herself to work that day and was still reeling from the shock of the announcement. Faith was acting distant and morose. Her conversation with Edwin had been nothing short of devastating. Faith had been so emotionally charged that Edwin could not get a word in edgeways and Naina had to finally pull her away from the phone and close the call. Nothing was going right!

Humming a rather sad, oldie-Goldie, Naina stared pensively at her monitor.

"Where the hell is Faith? It's so unlike her to be late for our project discussion. Well, what can I bloody expect at this time!" Naina called Faith on her mobile but Faith disconnected it. "Shit!"

Just then, Naina chanced to hear Surinder's low monotonous voice at pretty close quarters. She half turned around and, from the corner of her eye, saw him speaking to someone rather reticently. Naina had seen the man, with whom Surinder was standing with, before.

The stout yet striking man had a way about him. The crisp, white shirt and the neat gray trousers did nothing to conceal the careless abandon with which he carried himself. His face looked older than the 33 years that he was because of the dark circles that outlined his eyes and the sharp features that foretold of his stealthy nature.

An innocent bystander would not know that Dheer Choudherie was a force to be reckoned with at Stan Inc. He was politically powerful, morally corrupt, financially motivated and sexually dominating the higher strata of the company. Few people in the company had not heard of his escapades and even fewer remained who had not been entrapped in his snares. And everyone knew that Dheer had the goods on Chanchal. And anyone who had Chanchal in his court had already won the battle.

Piqued curiosity got the better of Naina and she got up to get closer to the action. She desperately wanted to eavesdrop on their conversation. Surinder had to be sharing privileged information with someone of Dheer's stature. Perhaps, Naina would get some inkling of why there were so many reporting changes being made just before such a crucial time for all of them.

Ordinarily, in such situations, they would call in additional quality/ operations resources for supporting the current operations guys. This way, the process improvement initiatives run by the quality experts would be augmented by the specialized business and process knowledge that the current operations managers would already possess. However, by changing operational reporting, Surinder was snatching away the process expertise from the whole approach. The new operations managers would need to run hatter scatter to grasp this knowledge in a short timeframe to be able to act effectively and really make a difference.

"So, let's find out what's really happening" thought Naina.

"Hey!" a voice called from behind Naina and she jerked back onto her seat.

"You scared me out of my wits! Are you alright?" whispered Naina animatedly

Faith eyed her with her typical "As if I care" look and changed the topic. "What mischief is the naughty Naina up to? I caught you listening in to Surinder. What's up now? Tell, tell."

"You interrupted me! I couldn't hear a thing. But I'm sure something major is coming our way. That's Dheer and if he's involved then it can't spell good things for us."

Naina explained to Faith what a piece of work Dheer was and the history behind this phenomenon at Stan.

Finally getting back to business, Faith ran through her project with Naina. This project was targeting a significant increase in accuracy levels in lieu of the customer mandate of 99% defects per unit of work done (DPU) in Naina's newly inherited process. The current levels of performance were at a 95% DPU, not bad but not too good either.

Faith had gotten into the "Quality" rhythm pretty quickly for someone so new in the system. Methodically, she reviewed the data that Naina had collected and something did not sit well with her. Instinctively, the numbers did not look right.

"This can't be right!" murmured Faith.

"What? What's the matter?" enquired Naina as she caught Faith frowning at the excel sheets.

"Who got you these numbers? Or did you extract these from the reporting system yourself?"

"These are the dashboards that Anita has been publishing for this process for the last six months. So, I thought we'd simply work off these."

"I want to see what the reports through out and compare those numbers to these figures. Can you get one of your trustworthy folks to do this for us?"

"Sure, I can. But, why do you want to do this? These dashboards are created from the data that the reports churn"

"Yeah, I know. But, my job is to ensure that that is actually the case!" and then Faith added, rather warily, "I have a dreary feeling that it just won't be"

✤✤✤

DAY 4

The Boardroom was buzzing with excitement. There were signs of another major news hitting the floor. Surinder was conversant and that was a surprise in itself. Ordinarily, he would sit in an ominous position around the oval table and just stare into his laptop. Today, he was almost cheerful and chatting freely with his managers. In light of the business changes, this was shocking, to say the least.

Suddenly, the loud chatter hushed and a solemn silence fell over. Dheer had made his entrance. He came round the conference table and sat himself down at the head. He then gestured for all to be seated. Everyone moved into his or her positions without as much as a word. Dheer then glanced in Surinder's direction that he took as his cue to begin the meeting.

"Thank you all for being here at such a short notice. I will not take too much of your time. I have important information to share with you. There are a few of you who have already come to guess what this could be." Surinder stopped here for emphasis before carrying on. "Due to the recent business exigencies that we have faced, the top leadership feels that I would be able to assist more in the capacity of a relationship manager. There is an immediate need for building bridges with the new leaders in the US and show them of what we have been able to achieve for them over the years and gain their trust. Also, CMort is currently going through its own challenges. To sustain the plan that we have set to resurrect our processes, we have the perfect candidate to help us through this journey. Please welcome Dheer who would now be taking my place as Assistant Vice President, Operations for the financial services vertical at Stan Inc."

There was a stunning silence, followed by a few managers daring to clap their acceptance. At which, Surinder decided to continue, "I understand that it would be a huge shock but let me assure you that this is best for all of us. Dheer brings with him extensive experience in client handling as well as process improvements. I will now leave the floor for Dheer to say a few words"

Dheer got up and walked to the head of the round table. He did not glance at anybody in particular but he noticed everyone. He saw everything: the apprehension, the anxiety, even fear. Oh! How he liked fear. And he knew exactly how to use that amazing human emotion to his advantage!

When he spoke, his voice was low yet surprisingly authoritative.

"I am a hard task master. I am a hard man to deal with. I *will* make your lives miserable. But, we will succeed. Any questions?"

Muted abeyance followed till one manager from the Vintage Group rose and asked this career-limiting question "How are you planning on taking us further on the 2-month deadline?"

"How long have you been in this process?" demanded Dheer

By this time, the manager had realized his gaffe. His reply came as a raspy breath "3 years"

"Would you then say that **you** are the subject matter expert and not I?" barked Dheer

"Yes"

"Then, *you* should tell me how we could increase our accuracy levels. Why are you asking me? Tell me what we should do and I'll get it done! Any other questions?"

There were none.

Chapter 2
ET TU, NAINA?

DAY 5

Naina had a one on one with dheer and after the previous day's display of dheer's boardroom-chairing capability; she wasn't quite looking forward to it. She knocked on his cabin door rather hesitantly and saw him, nod her in, from the glass partition.

He went back to something obviously more important, on his laptop, without as much as a second glance, as she stood inside his cabin unknowing what to do next. Uncertain, she continued to stand, feeling uncomfortable and annoyed at his lack of courtesy. Finally, after what seemed an eternity, he glanced in her direction and muttered, "Why are you standing there?" She took that as her cue to come over to the round table and settled in the seat farthest from him. Somehow she could tell that sitting as far away from him as possible would hold her in good stead through this meeting.

His cabin was as expected; impersonal and uncluttered. Most people had fairly messy desks to impress upon anyone who entered that they had a lot on their plates. Dheer, however, was a completely different animal. He did not need to exhibit his prowess; stories of his glamorous wins on generating new business, handling clients and completely turning around failing processes, had already done the office rounds and had gone down in Stan Inc. history. How did he do it all? No one had an inkling!

"I want you to work on something for me?"

The sudden interjection made Naina jerk out of her reverie. "I beg your pardon?"

"I repeat. There's an initiative I want you to work on."

"Sure! I would really like the opportunity to…" started Naina, only to be interrupted again.

"Yeah, OK. So, as you know we have a client satisfaction survey that we conduct bi-annually. I want you to coordinate it this time. And, if you do well, I would push you to Chanchal to lead e-VOC effort going forward."

Naina's eyes almost flopped out on hearing this. The e-VOC or the electronic Voice of Customer was an extremely critical part of third party operations. It fed into one of the business' key metrics on Client Satisfaction.

"Check your mail. I've sent you one on what needs to be done and whom to contact if you have any questions. Make it work!"

"Thanks" That's all Naina could fathom and once again, on cue, Naina made her move.

"Gosh!" Naina thought. If this was their first discussion, she could not imagine how working with him would be. He had not inquired about her career, so far, with Stan Inc or what her expectations were from him as her new boss. It was all about work. In a way, Naina respected that about him despite the crude monologue that she had just experienced.

And e-VOC would definitely provide her the leverage she needed to maybe get the next level that she had been vying for the last 1 year. She had worked very hard for it and this was an important step towards that goal.

"I'll do everything to get this right', she promised herself.

❀❀❀

Faith too had a taste of the rogue that was Dheer. Naina had had a gleeful look on her face that wholc day for some reason. Faith hadn't had a chance to speak to her about her one on one with Dheer and how that had gone. But considering Naina's expression, Faith had deduced that all was well in Naina-land.

Faith had been minding her own business at her desk when Dheer circled around the bay to stop right behind her. He began to flirt with the annoyingly cheerful manager – training, Preeti. At that point, Faith had not been introduced to Dheer but had obviously been a part of the boardroom announcement the previous day.

Bits of the conversation fell upon Faith's ears.

"Precisely, madam. It should be a simple task for you. I have noticed the great work that you have been doing since my last visit to this shop!" Dheer appreciated.

"Yes, I did turn over the training for the Mortgage exceptions process. Everyone has completed the entire set of soft skill trainings that I lined up for them. Do you remember that time when we got locked up in the elevator?" Preeti bragged

This got a naughty half smile to Dheer's face "Very vividly, madam."

Faith found what she heard a nuisance so she got back to her project but then she was interrupted.

"So, this is the enigma that people keep talking about." Dheer had turned to Faith but seemed to be talking more to him.

But Faith dashed out before she could check the words that passed her lips "I'm sure you've heard this from the wrong sect of society. To plebs, everyone looks an enigma!"

This amused Dheer as he retorted, "I'm sure there's nothing special here. But, just to be sure, there's a task that you might consent to undertake for me."

Faith was intrigued yet wished nothing more but to totally and absolutely refuse to take on any assignment from Dheer in any shape or form. She just did not like him yet she could not put her finger on what exactly it was about him that did it for her… or rather did not do it for her.

Unfortunately, she was now reporting to him indirectly and she was certain that anyone would be better than Surinder!

So, she conceded to take on the task.

"I will send you a mail. Go through it and prepare a strategy to conduct the next e-VOC survey. As you would know, it's extremely critical for us to get this right. Build a plan and share it in Chanchal's upcoming monthly review meeting."

All Faith could muster was a "Sure!" but she was beaming inside. "This is huge!" she thought to herself.

Neither of them knew then that they both had been given the same task by Dheer.

✤✤✤

DAY 12

Over the next week, Naina got fairly comfortable working with Dheer. He was pushy all right but he was fair. Everything had to be completed as of yesterday and he made no bones about his demands. One day, over coffee, Dheer made it clear to Naina that he would ensure she got promoted if she did exactly what he asked her to do and did it well.

Naina smiled and ensured Dheer that she would not disappoint him.

❦❦❦

Dheer was a quaint character. He ruled his direct reportees (DRs) by always keeping close tabs on the floor action. He double-checked on them and cross-questioned them. He gave them the impression that he was on their side whilst he only worked for his own gains all the way.

Over the short period that Naina had interacted with him, Dheer knew that she was an excellent manager. She had the potential to grow at Stan Inc. and god knew that she was due for her promotion. He also knew that to own her, he would need to own her career. But, he had his own outcome in mind for her. His sweet, little, devious mind.

❦❦❦

"Ah, the weekend!" exclaimed Faith. "How I love you, my precious. I wish Monday never comes"

Naina laughed at Faith's theatrics. The last week had been eventful. Dheer was a surprise package and she enjoyed having him as her boss. Naina believed that finally her journey with Stan Inc would change.

Faith was on her own trip. The results from the reporting audit on Naina's new process had come through and there were major discrepancies found in Anita's reporting and the actual data of the process. The flip side was that the process was in bigger shit than anyone had anticipated. The silver lining, however, was that Faith with Naina's help could put a concrete plan in place to finally discredit Anita and seek vengeance. How should they tell Dheer and Paul about Anita's misdemeanor? And, more importantly, when? If people could play games with them, they would outplay them. That was Faith's motto.

It was time for their Friday night dinner and long chat session. They had a lot to catch up on, as it had been a busy and eventful week.

As they settled comfortably in the lazy couches at the Fox, Faith noticed a familiar face and cringed. "Yikes! What is Dheer doing here?"

Naina was immediately concerned and looked around till she sighted him. She had come to realize that Dheer did not like Faith. In fact, he openly spoke about Faith with his DRs and none of it was complimentary. Naina had politely told Dheer a couple of time to stop bitching about Faith. She had made it very clear to him that Faith was her best friend and she certainly did not appreciate this hitting out at Faith.

In one of their regular dinner at Red Coral, a healthy debate was on between all the managers on team motivation. There was discussion around why and how to pep up your team members. All was well till Dheer deliberately touched the sensitive topic again...Faith.

'Her team is self motivated', He remarked. 'Her dressing sense is just so brilliant. With the skimpiest of clothes she wears, every guy is anyways eyeing her. They don't need any more motivation !', He laughed.

Naina who was about to take a bite into her favorite Chilli Chicken, stopped short and looked up at Dheer.

'Agreed Boss', added Akash, Dheer's favorite manager in another process. ' She's easy!', he winked.

Naina had kept her anger under control till then. Now she completely lost it.

'What the hell is wrong with you guys. Will you stop bitching about Faith. I've had enough of this nuisance.',

Naina barked. Her eyes were blazing with Fury with her face completely red with anger.

There was pin drop silence in the restaurant. Even people on the other tables turned around to look at what was happening.

'I've been continuously telling all of you how nice she is. If she's rich, is it her fault ? If she's attractive, is it her problem? But NO, you guys will not understand or actually do not want to understand. You know why ? Because your are jealous – of everything she has and you don't.'

And with that she got up and with one last look at Dheer left the restaurant.

Akash was shocked at Naina's outburst and so was Dheer but he pretended to be cool.

'The dinner is yummy ! Pass me the Crabs, will you', he asked Anita.

As she stood on the road looking for any public transport to get her back to office, she realized the impact of what she had just done.

'Dheer will screw my happiness', she told herself. 'Let him, I don't care a Damn. I couldn't have sat there listening to them bitch about my best friend.'

She came back to office and continued working.

She and Faith who was on leave that day had their routine good night call that night but she did not yet mentioned this to Faith for fear of causing her more stress.

It all came back to Naina when she spotted Dheer at Fox.

She instinctively ducked a little bit in her seat as she did not want to be seen dining out today. Faith had been low for some reason and had coaxed Naina to spare an hour for dinner at Fox in between the office hours. Naina could not say NO to Faith so she agreed.

She knew that Dheer was looking for reasons to pull her up for that night. He could get one today !

Faith, however had no clue about this. She recovered immediately after seeing Dheer and beckoned the waiter to order grub.

A toast to successfully completing Faith's project and a divine sip of wine later, Naina thought it best to start spilling the beans on Dheer. She had to warn Faith.

"I wanted to tell you something about Dheer.', and she began.

She told Faith how Dheer had told her to stay away from Faith, as she did not have a good reputation in the system and that it would affect Naina's chances for growth if she were associated with her. Also, that Dheer told one of his other managers that she was unprofessional and only rode on other people's achievements and did not contribute. In one of his DR meets, Dheer insinuated that he could get Faith if he chose to, whenever and wherever.

It was an hour before she stopped talking and Faith was fuming by then. She had listened to all that Naina told her and by the end of it was mad at Dheer ! 'I'll kill him', she hissed.

'Relax, there's more', replied Naina. 'He called me in his cabin yesterday and asked me to choose.'

'Choose What?', Faith questioned with a puzzled look.

'Between my Promotion and You.'

'WHAT ???', Faith was shocked

'Yeah, Crazy Bastard', Naina commented.

'And?'

'And What ? Do you need to ask me what I chose', Naina looked deep into Faith's eyes. Faith knew the answer.

In spite of all that Faith had had to put up with since she had joined Stan Inc., she was shocked to hear Naina. Dheer had interacted with her just a couple of times. She had also made tremendous progress on the e-VOC initiative and had shared a couple of excellent ideas to make it more effective.

"That two-faced bastard!" Faith cried out, furiously. "If he thought I was such a nincompoop, why did he ask me to lead the e-VOC survey this time around? What does he think of himself? That self-obsessed ass!"

Naina stopped Faith's tirades mid-way. "He asked you to work on the survey? Are you sure because I've been working on it the whole week myself? He asked me on Tuesday himself. He also told me if I did well, he would propose me leading the whole initiative going forward."

"Wait, wait, wait! He told me about this on Tuesday as well. Amazingly effective little contrivance, this! He's bloody playing with both of us!" Faith almost shrieked

This hit both of them but mostly Naina. But now she knew very well that he could do anything. Anything to get back at her...for refusing his promotion offer and choosing Faith. This had hurt his Ego and she knew that he would take revenge... Soon.

As Naina took a sip of her wine, a sudden realization hit her.

'Faith did not have any comment on how Dheer's been treating me. Its just not hit her ! And its only because of her that he now hates me. I have been openly fighting for her, taking *Pangas* with everyone. I have even given up my promotion for our friendship because I love her. And my suffering hasn't even registered with her!', she thought to herself as she gulped the wine in a go.

'We'll beat him at his own game', Faith continued. She had not realized that Naina had suddenly become very quite and it was not normal for her to change her mood.

'Strange…maybe she's too shocked to her about herself that my problems given by Dheer has not hit her as yet.', Naina sadly convinced herself. 'I wanted to discuss with her how I should guard myself now.. but will have to do it later… maybe some other day'.

There was a sudden lump in her throat. But she quickly recovered.

They continued with the dinner and general chit chat followed by their favorite ritual of scribbling on the bill and keeping it half-half.

Faith dropped her back in office. As she climbed the stairs up to the 2d floor, Naina was still thinking of Faith's reaction or the lack of it.

Her funda in life was simple. If I stand up for you, you do the same for me. Tit for Tat !

She had stood up for Faith. It was now Faith's turn to reciprocate.

✤✤✤

Naina tried to enter her home as discretely as she could. It was 3 am and she had had a little too much to drink.

She hoped that Dheer had not taken notice of them at Fox. Although Naina sincerely doubted that he believed that she would stop spending time with Faith specially after he had asked her not too and she had refused. They were chums and she would continue, as she was, irrespective of what Dheer thought of Faith. He had no business meddling in her private life.

Naina went straight into their bedroom but saw that the bed was not slept in. "Yash should have come in by now."

His flight had been delayed by 3 hours and Naina could not meet him before she left for work.

A little worried, Naina called Yash on his mobile. "Where are you?" she enquired urgently as he picked up.

"Hi Sweetheart! I'm at a friends' party. Remember the guy who sponsored my last show from Seagram's? I totally forgot to mention it to you."

This was not the first time Yash had forgotten about events that he needed to be at whenever he had a chance to be at home. This completely peeved Naina off. She hardly got any face time with her husband anymore and had never really adjusted to his social circle. She was a professional busy in her office always running a tight schedule and Yash was an extrovert who needed to be the center of attraction at all times. His job demanded that else his passion for concerts would have diminished.

"When would you be back home?" Naina asked knowing well that his answer would not corroborate his actual time of arrival.

'I'll be back in an hour. Why don't you go off to sleep. I'll wake you up when I reach home', She sighed as she heard his noncommittal response and kept down the phone.

Her happy high was gone and there was something nagging at her chest. It was the same feeling she got whenever Yash got back home from his travels. Is this how marriages turn out after a few years? Spending time apart becomes critical to unwind and de-stress from when you are together? Or maybe she was reading in it too much ? Had she ignored Yash in her friendship with Faith ?

She did not have answers to these questions.

Naina had let others rule her emotionally for as long as she could remember. Now that she thought about it, Faith had become critical to her. She could provide her the peace, solace and happiness that she needed from a friend.

Earlier, she used to be ecstatic only when she was painting but human interaction with someone who could understand you completely was so redeeming.

Yash and Naina had somewhat drifted apart and she desperately wanted to bring her married life back on track.

'I need to spend more time with him. Maybe he's lonely and feels left out without me specially while he's traveling', she told herself.

And with that thought, she switched off the lights and went off to sleep.

She dreamt of her being thrown into water and shouting for help as water seeped through her lungs. She did not know how to swim. Far on the shore, were some familiar faces though she couldn't recognize. They saw her struggling but didn't jump in to help. They kept giggling as they chatted amongst themselves.

Suddenly a hand came towards her and she was lifted up into a boat. She looked deep into those eyes that had melted her heart a few years ago. As he hugged her, she knew she was safe…safe in Yash's arms.

✱✱✱

DAY 15

The following Monday, when Dheer called Faith in his cabin, Faith's ill-concealed animosity for Dheer became rather worse concealed. She had half a mind to confront him with whatever Naina had told her but Naina would've freaked out and she did not want to wreak Naina's chances of a promotion. She understood what that meant to Naina and how much effort she had put into her work in the last 3 years to get where she had.

"So, how's your project going?"

Faith briefed him about her findings and updated him on the bare facts that she planned on sharing with Edwin that evening. But, she did not tell him about Anita's data fudging that she had come by. That piece of news she would save for later.

Faith had a call with Edwin in a couple of hours on the progress made on her project and that was the only thing that was keeping her going through the day.

"Ok. And the e-VOC?" Dheer went back to something on his laptop.

Faith frowned at this. She thought it rude and discourteous to stare at your laptop while conversing with someone but then what else could be expected from this maniac. "We have completed the plan. Naina hasn't arrived at the office yet. Her process will begin in another two hours. When she comes in, we will run you through it together."

Dheer's head snapped back as he glanced directly at her "Naina and you are working on it together? Who asked you to do that?" he glowered.

Faith played it cautiously and responded innocently "I think you've forgotten that both of us have been working on this for the past week. Well, we thought 2 minds together would be so much better."

"Hmm. Good then. Bring her in and we'll discuss it" and, with that remark, Faith was dismissed.

Faith and Naina had come up with this plan together the previous evening. Naina had already developed it to a large extent as she already had significant knowledge on the subject and had been working very hard on it. They had, however, wanted Dheer to get the impression that they were working in tandem and completely as a team.

When Naina came in, they shared the plan with Dheer and he seemed to really like it. He appreciated it even. It was efficient and covered all the bases.

"Shall we put this in a pitch for Chanchal's review then?" enquired Faith as creating a PowerPoint presentation for a formal review was the norm.

"No. No need for a pitch at all. I want it to be a discussion where you run us through your ideas and we build on those through the meeting.", replied Dheer.

Faith was a little relieved, as she believed that preparing pitches was one of the biggest wastes of time and energy. She could, however, do an excellent job with them as she had demonstrated in the past. She was looking forward to the review the next day as this could also spell of better things to come for her career.

✾✾✾

DAY 16

'Answer the phone Dammit', Naina hissed. She had been trying Faith mobile now for more than an hour. Faith wasn't picking it up.

'God knows whats wrong with her phone. And I don't even have her residence number.'

Naina was desperately trying to reach Faith. She had to share an important information with her.

Dheer had called Naina in the morning and told her to come two hours early to work.

'Its important. I need some urgent information for an upcoming client and I have to prepare a pitch for them. I need you to provide me with some data about Mortgage.', he told her.

'Sure, whats it about', she asked.

'Come over. I'll tell you when we meet', he instructed and hung the phone.

Naina was puzzled. Still she didn't try to read too much into his call.

'Lets go and find out', she told herself. 'And lemme also tell Faith.' She then looked into her watch.

12pm. 'Madam would be sleeping right now. *Chalo*, I'll call her from work.', she decided and got ready to go to work.

Dheer had called her two more times by the time she reached office. She had chosen not to answer his calls. He was waiting for her when she reached office. She went to his cabin directly.

'Yes Dheer. Tell me, what data do you want', she asked him.

'Naina, I just spoke to Chanchal. He wants to see how would we roll out the e-VOC Survey', Dheer told her.

'Ya, so we are going to talk about it today in the review. Faith and I are prepared.', Naina assured him. She was also surprised that this was the reason for Dheer to be nearly frantic in his calls to her today.

'No No. You are not understanding my point. He wants you to pitch out the same. A visual presentation would be much more effective. Besides it'll bring across your point much better if you do it on the screen', he answered.

'Okay. But we have just an hour left. Have you called Faith as yet ?', she asked him.

'No, I couldn't get the time. Why don't you make the presentation here and once Faith is in, you can show her. It'll save time.', he instructed. 'Here, sit down in my cabin and make it in front of me.

Dheer did not allow Naina to go out of his room. He was very well aware that Naina would have immediately called Faith to update her on this new development which he did not want her to.

Naina found it strange that he had only called her…several times actually but had not called Faith. It was a disturbing thought, but she didn't analyze it.

Naina trusted everyone she met…almost everyone. This was another *Funda* of her life – Trust until Betrayed. Then she would not forget or forgive. But such a trusting person she was, she did not think that there could be any hidden agenda in this move by Dheer.

'Must be his stupid Ego. He anyways tries to throw attitude around her...That's why he couldn't probably bring himself to call her', she answered her question herself.

'I'll call Faith', she told Dheer.

'Listen Naina, I want you to start working on this RIGHT NOW ! Do you understand ? Call her afterwards.' Dheer replied rudely.

'Bastard', she murmured under her breath and glanced at her watch. It was 2pm. The review would start at 3.

'I have only an hour left. Let me prepare a basic two slide pitch. I'll share it with Faith once its done and then add whatever she suggests', Naina decided. She knew Faith would reach office only at about 2.45 pm. She would start from home at 2.30pm as she lived close by.

Naina prepared the pitch in about half an hour and showed it to Dheer. He gave a go ahead.

Naina rushed out of Dheer's cabin and started dialing Faith's number. There was no answer.

Naina came back into the present. She had no other way to contact Faith. She could only wait for Faith.

The review was starting in 5 minutes and there was no sign of Faith.

✾✾✾

It was a little daunting to sit in a 10-seat meeting room with all the top notches of your Center of Excellence. Naina was confident of the plan but was very uneasy. Faith had not come in as yet and neither could she contact her. She wanted to tell Faith about the pitch and run it past her before the review so that they could pitch it together.

But there was no choice now. Naina had to do it alone!

As the review started with Chanchal giving some updates about the COE and some planned Client visits in the coming week. He was in the middle of his talk, when Faith appeared.

All heads turned towards the entrance where she stood.

"I am so sorry Guys. I got caught in a VIP traffic Jam and couldn't make it on time', Faith spoke.

'That's alright Faith. Come in', Chanchal waved at her to join them. Faith Sat down at the closest seat available. She looked around and found Naina in an extreme corner. Her face was red and she was staring at Faith.

'What's wrong with Nain. I just got a little late', she looked at Naina with a puzzled look.

Naina was red with anger. 'Here I am so desperately trying to reach Faith and there she is so casual and relaxed about it. I am sure her phone is on 'Mute' and she hasn't even bothered to look at it. How will she know that I have called so many times?', she thought.

'All right Team. That's all that I wanted to share.', Chanchal ended his update' Whose coming next', he questioned.

Dheer stood up and addressed the group. "The e-VOC survey is critical to all our businesses. Historically, the way it has been planned has had a lot to be desired. We have seen clients being missed out, lack of complete process coverage, incorrect collation of response data and I could go on. I, therefore, felt that this needed to be looked at procedurally. My manager Naina will be heading this initiative supported by Faith from a quality perspective. Naina, if you could take the group through the proposal"

Faith took a moment to completely understand what had happened. She physically shook her head a little. Her mind was buzzing with thoughts. "What! I would be supporting Naina and she would head it?" Faith knew how much she had contributed to the plan.

Just then, she saw a presentation on their plan pull up on the projector. Faith was shocked beyond belief. "When was this made?" she wondered. The last she knew was Dheer negating the need to create one.

Faith was shocked ! Presentation ??? She couldn't understand.

Naina stood up from her chair and walked towards the screen. As she walked past Faith, she whispered, 'Come with me'.

Faith did not move. It was as if she was frozen in time … as if her feet had been rooted to the floor.

Naina looked at her again and Faith turned her face away. She was blazing with Anger.

'How could she have done this to me ? When did she make this and why didn't she tell me ? How could she… ?'

There were a lot of unanswered questions in her mind that only Naina could answer. But Faith knew that Naina would have no answer that could justify this move.

It was simple. Naina had betrayed her, She had traded their friendship for her promotion.

Naina and Dheer had made her look like a complete idiot as she had been taken for a ride.

No one messed with Faith Jones and got away with it. That, she ensured!

Chapter 3

"FAITH"LESS ASSERTIONS

DAY 16

Faith was furious, and justifiably so. Naina had tried to reason with her but had failed miserably.

Faith, Please allow me to explain *Yaar*', Naina pleaded to her. She knew Faith was very hurt.

She desperately need to explain everything to Faith. The reality…as it was.

But Faith was in no mood to listen.

'There was so little she can say to explain herself. Dheer must have put a lot of pressure on her to create that pitch and she did. Her future depends on getting credit for making that plan. She has done…perhaps unwillingly, as Dheer had asked of her. Now she's regretting it.', Faith thought.

'Shit, How do I explain to this silly girl, what actually happened. That I too am a victim and not the back-stabber as she thinks I am', Naina was in pain. A lot of emotional pain as she was being shunned by her best friend.

Faith had gone to Barista to cool off. She returned to her seat after an hour only to find an apology note in her mail. She deleted it without a second glance and grimly went back to working on her project. She was in Analyze, which is the most challenging phase of the project where one runs statistical tests on identified potential key causes for the problem. This forms the basis for building improvement plans to resurrect failing metrics and attain project goals.

Just as she successfully directed her full attention to the Moods Median test that she was about to perform, she heard Devyani demand, "Faith, I need to speak to you".

Devyani was a petite and pretty Punjabi girl who was a great mix of street smarts and innocence. There was a kick-ass attitude about the lass that Faith appreciated and could relate to.

Faith recognized immediately a sense of urgency in her ordinarily sweet, mellow voice. Devyani was working with Faith on her project as a team member and valued that exposure immensely. She had developed a high level of respect for Faith and found it comforting to divulge all her inner thoughts and emotions to her role model.

"Sure, babe! Whazzup?"

"Can we go to Barista for a chat?"

"Of course! It seems I'll be getting more than my fair share of coffeeista today" Faith kidded to lighten Devi's mood. Devi, which means Goddess in Hindi, was a nickname that Faith had popularized for Devyani. Now, everyone who knew her in the company called her by that, much to her chagrin.

Faith settled at the coffee table with another glass of her favorite cold coffee, Barrrista whilst Devi indulged in an apple pie. "*Haanji, toh ab bata ki kya hua jo itna urgent hai*" ("Yes madam, so now tell me what's happened that's so urgent?")

"I didn't want to shock you so I did not call you yesterday night. Otherwise I have been dying to tell you this"

Faith got concerned on hearing her begin the way she did. She got a dreary feeling about what she was about to hear. But she could never prepare herself for what she ultimately did.

"But, how can it be possible?" she wondered. She knew Devyani well and she would have no reason to tell her what she did except to vent. She would never make up something like this.

But, this was big! No, huge!!

The top brass along with a few of the managers would have to be involved in this racket. And that was exactly what it was, a racket.

She comforted Devi yet urged her to come forward with this information to Chanchal. But, like any prudent person, she did not want to divulge. However, she wanted justice. And Faith knew just how to get her that!

DAY 22

Over the next week, a wild rumor spread across the entire floor: A completely unbelievable crazy rumor that anyone who passed it on to his confidante could, himself, not believe it entirely.

Especially for CMort, and the Vintage Group, it was a trying time, as one of them had been targeted. Vicki Manchanda was alleged to have taken a *broad* from his process to an empty apartment on the way to dropping her home after a process party. This, he accomplished, on the premise that he needed to check out that apartment for renting it. Also, he was not the only one who had taken this very same girl to that apartment. There was another manager of the Vintage Group who had done this before and, thus, the girl realized that there was something fishy. She demanded to be dropped home immediately or she would scream "molestation!"

What was unbelievable about this story was that Dheer was insinuated. And that he had been caught with his pants down with his favorite team member, in that very apartment.

Faith knew that the rumor was absolutely true and she also knew that she was the one who had passed on this brilliant piece of news to the blabbermouth Anita under the uttermost secrecy.

Now, it was time to take care of Anita herself. She had done enough damage in the system to deserve any sympathy from Faith.

***

Dheer heard of the rumor and blasted Vicki and the other manager for mishandling their personal matters. He wanted to get to the bottom of how this got leaked out and who was the person responsible for spreading it.

Dheer was in control and he knew nothing could touch him. After all, Chanchal was the final point of contact for anyone who would wish to raise an integrity concern against him and he was confident that the closure of such concerns would happen in his favor.

After all, Chanchal owed him. He had really liked the apartment too, you see.

Chapter 4
PERIOD OF REDEMPTION

DAY 22

Naina was being given the silent treatment and she hated it. Faith always did this when she was upset. She had this knack of completing withdrawing into her shell and making the other person feel like shit!

She had to end this row of self-pity and reason with her. Everyone makes mistakes and her mistake was that she didn't insist on calling Faith before making the Presentation. But she wanted faith to understand her perspective. That she did it under pressure. She never even once thought of betraying Faith.

And she wanted to correct whatever happened. She would involve Faith in the e-VOC initiative or perhaps confront Dheer and tell him that Faith truly deserved to lead it. She would figure something out.

She called Faith on her mobile and got a cold "Hello".

"Come on, *yaar*. Let's talk about it at least."

"I thought that we did that already. How can you further explain yourself? I don't need to hear more."

"I understand how you feel but you know Dheer and how he can create so much pressure that you can balk. He can make my career here and we both know how important that is to me.

Finally, after years, I have found someone who can path the way for me. Plus, I will make it up to you. I promise. I will tell Dheer that you should lead this initiative and not I."

"Look Naina. Don't you dare do such a thing! Unlike you, I do not need anybody's support but my own grit to push my case forward. I know how to fight for myself. You might have won round 1 but I assure you that I will win the war!"

"Hey! This is not our fight. Don't suck us into this, Ok?"

"It's totally our fight now. And *I* haven't sucked us into anything. Or do I have to remind you?" barked Faith

Naina was tired of feeling guilty over her little mistake. She was also angry at Faith for not understanding her and hitting where it hurt the most…her career. But she was mature enough to understand Faith's perspective and she wanted them to work together to resurrect their friendship as before. Faith, of course, was not yet ready to move on. She was still hurting. Naina did not want to confront that aspect. She had not understood Dheer's motives and the impact of what that one mistake of not calling Faith before making the presentation could do. She had tried calling so much that day after all. Maybe it was destined to be this way.

Naina gave in once again and closed the call on a very agitated and irate Faith.

DAY 25

Dheer was not overtly fond of Anita as there was no real love lost between Surinder and Dheer. Dheer also made it extremely clear to Anita that she was operating in rough terrain.

With Dheer's focus shifting to the Apartment Controversy, Faith knew his fuse would be shorter than usual and this would be the opportune time to blow the game open on Anita. Faith was a woman on a mission.

In Dheer's first team review, Faith added an agenda item for discussion on her project. She was sure that Dheer would not object because this would definitely give him ammunition to cross-question Faith on her approach and project results.

As Faith entered the Boardroom, she caught Naina looking at her. She immediate directed her gaze to another black belt who ordinarily stole every opportunity to make eyes at her. Shantanu was only a few weeks into the process but was already playing the snakes and "ladder" game. However, he did not yet know that Faith had him wrapped around her little finger and he could not work his tricks on her. Shantanu smiled at Faith that Faith reciprocated, only, the smile did not touch her eyes and remained a tight line set across her face. She had to play this game very deftly and, although she commended herself on her performance so far, she wasn't intrinsically made to play these games.

With Paul in conference for this meeting, Dheer began the performance review, process by process. The results weren't encouraging given the stringent timelines set for improvements. Naina's process especially was scrutinized the most due to the high client focus and criticality. Anita along with Naina was put on the spot equally as Naina had essentially inherited Anita's miss-management.

Dheer had taken away Naina's original process from her and given her Anita's which was in a mess, both process and people management. She knew that he had done this deliberately a week before the review so that she gets all the blame for it. She had inherited the process about a week back and was deep-diving into it to dig out the pain areas. That Faith was not helping out in this,became a bigger challenge from a time management perspective.

And then came Faith's chance to walk the ramp. She presented her project with great ease and emphasized well on the core findings. Yet, nothing that she spoke was extremely enlightening.

So, Dheer commented, "Well, this is all ok. But, what is it that you have really dug out. We all knew that updates management has been an issue. The repository does not get refreshed in time and people rarely look at the knowledge portal in case they have queries. We know that the critical Xs are people, tenure, productivity pressures, lack of controls. So, what else?"

Faith answered, "Please add to that miss-reporting of data and integrity issues on elevating process performance significantly over the actual results"

There was a sudden murmur of activity going round the room followed by a stunned silence.

Paul was himself going berserk on the call asking for a repeat of what had occurred. He, as usual, would have switched his mind to his churning his mails in the interim.

Faith repeated herself with her gaze fixed on a very perturbed Anita whose face rapidly turned colors and finally decided to close on an unbecoming shade of green as Faith took the entire line of managers and leadership through her entire gamut of findings.

Dheer composed himself through the tirade of assertions and barked at Naina. "Did you know about this?"

Naina found herself nodding. 'I got to know this couple of days ago when I started digging in. but I wanted to be sure before I could jump to conclusions.', Naina justified herself.

Dheer and Paul then quickly closed the meeting and called Anita in, separately, to discuss the matter. Last Faith heard, Anita had put in her papers and flicked all CMort proprietary process documentation with her to one of Stan Inc's competitors. She was blacklisted from Stan and HR was intimated never to hire her again.

***

Meanwhile, Naina was beginning to feel left out. Faith was not speaking with her; Anita had left under the direst circumstances and had been upset with Naina for not helping her out. After all, they had been close for so long. The Vintage Group managers had banished Naina from their kingdom when she had chosen to befriend Faith.

Naina had found out about the discrepancies in the process data a day after she took over the handover from Anita. After all she was the process expert. Her instincts told her where to dig and she found huge data mis-management and duplicate entries in the system. She knew it was a huge blunder. This could cost them the entire business…specially in these circumstances.

Naina knew that anyone who brings this out would be in the limelight. She had an idea.

She decided to rope in Faith to do the analysis and get the credit for highlighting this huge gap. This would also give the leadership the necessary and desperately required confidence in Faith's image as a good performer as Dheer had made a huge mess of it already.

But there was a problem.

She knew that Faith would not support her now as she was pissed off at the e-VOC incident. Neither would she take a so called favor from Naina. Stubborn as she was.

Naina called one of her team lead Bharti.

'Bharti, Listen to me carefully. I want you to go to Faith with this data and tell her that you need help in analyzing it.

Tell her that I have given you a Root Cause Analysis to do but I do not have the time to sit with you. So you have decided to go to Faith as she's an expert who can guide you. Ask her to look at the data. She'll figure out the rest herself', Naina explained the plan to Bharti.

Naina knew she could trust her.

Bharti did as told and suddenly Naina saw Faith spending more time in her process and with her people. Her plan had worked.

Faith was right on the verge of revealing one of the biggest misses at Stan Inc.

Faith was not sharing information with Naina on her improvement plans and was taking her ideas straight to Naina's direct reportees for implementation. This started bugging Naina eventually as she felt she was losing her span of control over her own team members. There were still so many fixes to implement, the process was in a mess and there was a long way to reach their targets and not too long to go till the 'D' day.

She decided it was time for a professional confrontation with Faith. She just had to tell her how things would be done in her process from now on. She found Faith taking a call in one of the small meeting rooms lining the floor. She took the liberty of walking right in.

Faith had her back to the door and did not see Naina enter. Faith was concentrating hard on what was being said on the call. Naina recognized the voice as Edwin's and remembered that Faith had a project review call with him. As she turned back to exit the room, she heard something that she just had to stay for.

"Dheer told me Naina's process is not progressing as it should be. And I attribute it to her mismanagement if, in spite of your project and action plans, she's not able to turn around her performance."

To Naina's surprise, Faith supported her and relayed the whole process background of a history of mishandling.

"But Dheer made me believe that Naina has made it worse since she took over"

"Edwin, trust me, Naina has made a huge difference in team morale. The number are actually better than before. The performance metrics are looking worse only because this is the first time in years that the actual data is being reported. I'm surprised that Dheer did not inform you of Anita's misconduct and departure from Stan."

Faith elaborated on the recent events for Edwin's benefit. He started to see the real game but was surprised that Dheer had deliberately tried to indict Naina.

Naina stood inside the meeting room in shock. All her illusions about Dheer vanished in that instant. "What would he have to gain from this?", she wondered but she got no response.

Faith brought Edwin on board with everything that was happening at CMort, India so that he could now have a clearer picture of their progress. As she finished with the call and turned around, she saw Naina standing at the door. She had a somber look on her face that foretold of her emotions.

"Hey, look. Just because I'm upset with you don't mean I'm not going to support you." Faith chided Naina.

"Thanks. And when the hell were you going to tell me that you and Edwin are alright again!" scolded Naina right back.

'Dinner?', Faith suggested.

'Yes! Where?', Naina asked, relieved that Faith was responding.

'*Aur Kahan* (where else), Fox but of course', Faith replied. She finally smiled.

They were sitting at their favorite table along the window overlooking the garden. Kevin and his band was playing. There was music everywhere. The settings couldn't have been better!

They cleared all their misunderstandings and patched up.

"Well… he called and I listened', Faith began. 'Edwin really isn't against Stan Inc. He had his reasons and they were fine by him but I also talked and he listened. He realizes now that nothing will be gained by taking the business back. 800 people would be jobless and no one would gain by it in the US. So, we must right whatever has been mishandled and erect the operations like they should have, in the first place. He will back us up", explained Faith.

"That's great! But, does Dheer know of this?"

"Well, Dheer and everyone else already thinks that Pam had given them a real chance for the two months' deadline. They did not realize that that was a ploy while they made back-up plans to support the business. Although Edwin always knew that it would be a formidable task to upscale, by 100% of the task force present with us, back in the US. They would have had to run parallel operations for at least another 6 months, post the final decision to pull back"

Naina seemed like finally things were going their way. She relaxed and requested for their favorite number to be played.

As Kevin toasted 'Nothings gonna change my love for you' to them, they raised their wine glasses in acknowledgement.

Naina could now work full steam ahead to bring her process right up! And handle Dheer from the forefront…

Besides Faith and she were together back again…

✽✽✽

DAY 30

Faith's project moved into the next stage of the lifecycle: Improve. This is when she had thought that she would face the most challenge. Improve meant suggesting improvements and getting them approved from the likes of Dheer and Paul would take a huge amount of effort. She would have to leverage Edwin to push her case forward. Naina's project had begun to yield benefits already. Her attrition was lowest in the business for the previous month and the process accuracy already looking up.

Faith had once again started involving Naina in her improvement plan because she was the one who would have to implement them post approval.

Naina had an amazing control over her people. They cherished her as their manager and looked up to her for advice.

The rumors about the business going back had started doing the office rounds amongst even the agent levels and there was a high amount of anxiety building in the ranks.

Naina took a process huddle to alleviate these rumors. Sometimes, managers have to overtly lie in order to control a mass hysteria. Because of her open and transparent relationship with her team members, they believed her when she really needed them to. There were so many changes happening around them that, in these times of uncertainty, even the most loyal employees start thinking of skipping ship. But, they didn't and all because of her leadership abilities and all-out support.

As she stepped out of her huddle, Dheer motioned her to follow him to his cabin. Naina was furious with him after what she had learnt earlier in the week. However, he could be an insolent rogue at work and she still did not want to irk him.

"Naina, what did I tell you about Faith? Stay away from her. If you wish to make your career here, start listening to what I direct you to do"

"What does my friendship with Faith have to do with you or my next level?" she demanded

"No one likes Faith. They think that all you both do is sit around and twiddle your thumbs over coffee."

As Naina retaliate before Dheer could stop her in her tracks. " I've told you before Dheer. There is no choice here. We've discussed this in the past and you know what I chose before.', Naina raised her voice.

"Do as I tell you. OK? Now, I have to work"

"No Dheer, If you tell me this again, believe me, I'll escalate at Chanchal's level', she openly threatened him.

Naina then left his room fuming but she knew he would not take this lying down.

DAY 40

Naina had a few friends in the support functions still. The IT manager, Ranit, for CMort, was a 35-year-old veteran, stuck at the Manager level. He had been victimized by Chanchal's whiplash of a tongue on many occasions.

Ranit came to her seat one day and took her aside. He wanted to highlight an integrity case in her process, where one of her team leaders was sending out privileged information and Standard Operating Procedures outside the company.

This is a serious offence by any standards and Naina had to immediately highlight this to Dheer, who did not take it well.

"Why doesn't anyone man your floors? Haven't I told you to be more attentive for your processes before?" he barked at Naina, in front of Ranit.

Naina started to explain but he stopped her short. "I do not want to listen to excuses. I will have to raise it to Chanchal and he will not take it kindly. Go and prepare a plan to handle this and then wait for further instructions"

Naina was furious on tears as she walked outside Dheer's cabin.

Ranit was one who got to be in a lot of meetings that Chanchal held for his direct reportees and, thus, got to hear the inside workings of the lot. He warned Naina that she should stay away from Faith.

"Why are you also telling me that?" Naina inquired.

"Alright, don't tell anyone I told you this but Dheer told Chanchal that Faith and you aren't close at all and he will ensure that that remains true. This is because Chanchal does not want the culture he has created to become homely and friendly and uncompetitive"

"What the… this is ridiculous? Our friendship has gone to Chanchal's level? This has to be Surinder's doing! Crazy!"

"Crazy, yes. But true. When I heard it, I could not believe people at these levels can be so frivolous but they can", explained Ranit.

Naina called Faith immediately and relayed this input. She also told Faith that because she had started answering Dheer back, he was now seeking revenge and had started making her life at work, a living hell.

Faith was at her nerve's end and could only offer Naina solace. "Do you think we should ease off taking breaks and being seen working too much together?

"Are you crazy? That's totally not the solution. But, Faith, I do not understand what they have against you!"

"I think it's Surinder's first impression and, since I am doing good work, they can't chuck me. For Dheer, it is totally the apartment incident and, who knows, perhaps even Chanchal is involved. What say?"

"Yeah, Faith. I think you've taken on too many enemies at the start of your career here"

"Babe, I'm more worried about you. I don't care and it doesn't affect me as much"

"Neither does it me. A true friendship is ever more important"

And so they decided to carry on as they were... in spite of raging negativity from all quarters.

DAY 45

It had taken Faith an entire week to get her process improvement proposal approved. With only 2 more weeks to go, she had limited time. She wondered if they would have ever approved it if Edwin had not reminded them of the eventuality of a stalled project in the midst of these times.

It was a comprehensive plan for CMort as a business and she had called an emergency 2 hour-long meeting to discuss the implementation with all the operations managers. She had predicted opposition and, therefore, she had invited Paul as well as Edwin on conference. She had capped her sides well and defended the questions extremely well. The timelines were rigid and extreme, to say the least, but everyone had to agree what with Paul and the client listening in.

Faith and Naina had to keep a tight control on the goings on for the next 2 weeks. Although, operationally, all the MIS glitches had been resolved and the numbers for the metrics had looked back for the first few weeks but they were steadily on the rise now and looked good.

DAY 57

The dashboard review call:

There was nervousness all-around. Even though they had performed, there was an element of uncertainty in the air.

The review began with Edwin taking about his India trip and how he had come to know of the data mismanagement. He then continued to describe the reviews afterwards and the efforts to clean up the mess by the India team.

Finally Pam spoke. 'A 30% increase in productivity along with significant improvements in accuracy had been observed. I haven't seen a better turnaround in my entire career ! And that too in a span of two months! Congratulations to all of you. The process stays!'

Edwin and Pam raved about the obvious turnaround. Much to Dheer's chagrin, Pam offered a special compliment to both Faith as well as Naina's projects on their successful completion.

Pam had decided that with such amazing results, Stan Inc. could indeed make a huge difference in the future as well. She was amazed at Naina's Operational management and now had Faith too in the new leadership team to carry on running the business. Furthermore, there was hope still for additional business. Edwin would keep a close eye and continue to review their progress for future opportunities.

As the call ended, there was jubilation and backslapping. Faith and Naina hugged each other and were also, surprisingly, congratulated by the others in the group.

It was a time for their celebration at their favorite haunt, the Fox.

It was a beautiful night and a happy ending to a painfully long journey. Abut it had been worth it. They had learnt a lot and had both emerged as winners from it.

Much to their own surprise, they danced together for the first time at Fox. Both of them dead drunk, danced away to glory……

<u>PART SEVEN</u>

THE GRANDE ANNOUNCEMENT

Shivraj Thukral, the founder and CEO of Stan Inc. was a brilliant and formidable man. A man with the gift of the gab and a powerful orator, everyone at the annual company town hall waited with baited breath to hear what he had to say.

The Yearly Town Hall was an event where the wins of the past year were celebrated, plans for the future shared and the most awaited Diamond Award bestowed upon a few outstanding players.

Three months had passed since that fateful day when they had retained CMort back.

The business was back in shape and was running fine. Faith was mentoring bigger projects whereas Naina had been given additional processes to manage. Their career was booming.

A cultural program initiated the town hall and, this year, Naina and Faith had led the organizing committee. The event featured items from nominated team members from each business process. Naina and Faith had something up their sleeves this year.

The two ladies in question were backstage, prepping the young crowd of participants. There were around 60 Stan Inc employees engaged. Naina noticed that Faith was slightly edgy and pre-occupied. "What's up with you today? Our guys will do great!"

"Oh, I know. It's just I hope you get the Diamond Award for the biggest turnaround that a process has seen."

"Well, you know I want it bad! In fact, I wanted to tell you earlier but I spoke to Yash and, if I don't get the award, I will quit!"

"What? Are you crazy, Nain? I know you really deserve it and you've given a lot of yourself to this business over the last three years but isn't this a little abrupt? I do wish you would re-consider this decision."

"No yaar. I've waited to get this award for two years in a row and, god knows, I've earned it!"

"Well, let's not think pessimistic. I'm sure Chanchal and Dheer would have considered you. There's no one else to nominate."

"I'm somehow not that hopeful but you never know"

The event began with a beautiful MC cheering the crowd on.

"Without further ado, we have just one cultural program this year as opposed to several items, each presented by different businesses. So, please welcome Stan Inc. cultural team. Faith & Naina, all yours!"

The lights dimmed but when they lit up again, they were focused center-stage on two figures clad in all black. Chanchal, Dheer and Paul sat alongside Shivraj and stared as they all realized that the two ladies were Faith and Naina. The entire dance had been choreographed by them and as it progressed the entire audience was spellbound. All 60 associates along with Faith and Naina gyrated to the rhythm of "One Love".

When they climaxed into the finale, Stan Inc applauded their performance like no other. Never before had the leadership participated and danced along with the agents and, all of them took bows, amidst whistles and claps.

Faith and Naina hugged each other as they met back-stage. "It was amazing!" "Fab!" "Great job, babe!" "It worked, Faith!!! Did you see the looks of Chanchal and Dheer?" They giggled.

"This has been the best night of my life" exclaimed Naina. "Ditto, babe!" screamed Faith.

As they cheered backstage, the rewards ceremony had begun. Shivraj shared the business wins of the previous year and applauded CMort for the amazing turnaround, for which he thanked all those associated with the improvements.

In the manager's category, he began to read out the citation for the winner of the Diamond Award. "This tremendous player has upheld the values that Stan Inc has always stood for: Passion and Integrity and continuous Client Satisfaction! Having successfully completed a high impact, upscale business improvement project, this person not only has significant achievements in strategic initiatives but also employee retention. Please congratulation the winner of the Diamond Award for this year, Naina Chopra!"

As the name reverberated through the auditorium, Naina felt elevated. She could not believe it. Still, she could not believe it. Could she get happiness too ? Yes, she could and she had ! Naina ran up the stairs onto the stage to receive her beautiful Glass Trophy along with a check of rs.1 lac. She waved at Naina from the stage who was waving back at her with both hands.

'Congrats baby...This deserves Champagne !', Faith screamed as she held Naina's trophy in her hands.

'Yeah, it does. Lets go and party', Naina suggested.

" Lets not go yet. There's more" is all that Faith told her. Then turned her attention back on Shivraj. Naina followed her with a puzzled look.

'More?'

Shivraj was talking about a personal investment that he made in the company six months earlier.

Naina carried on though. "Faith, I'm so happy today that I want to finally do what I have been wanting to for sometime now.

'What?'

'Resign', Naina replied coolly.

'*KYA* ?, have you gone nuts ? Why would you resign? You've won the best performer award for the year. I am sure your promotion is coming!', Faith was shocked at Naina's decision.

'Ya, its true. I always wanted this promotion and I know that now I will certainly get it. But you know what? Now that I have achieved what I wanted to, I don't want it. I just wanted to prove myself to mom…and specially to Dad. That I will make it big someday. Now I want to focus on my personal life…to spend time with Yash, to play with Randy, to be with mom. And to Paint. Faith I want to PAINT !." Naina looked so peaceful. Finally she was, with herself.

"Nain, you should do whatever would make you happy. Listen, honey, Shivraj is about to make an announcement that should not change anything between us."

"What? Faith, nothing can change us or my love for you. Why did you say that?

And then Naina heard Faith's name being called on. "Faith? Can we please have you on stage?"

Faith winked at Naina who looked confused. As Faith walked up, Shivraj continued. "Faith is my daughter. With a strong educational background and tremendous experience in the financial services industry, she is more than equipped to take on the baton from me. However, I'm still too young to retire", chided Shivraj. That extracted laughter from the stunned audience, especially that belonged to CMort. "With this, I give you the COO of Stan Inc.: Faith Jones"

Faith graciously took the spot and spoke her thanks and how she would conduct the business, what her values were and how important employee satisfaction was to Stan Inc. She had taken the time to know Stan Inc. from the grass root level up and knew what she needed to fix. She directed her gaze at Chanchal, Dheer and Paul as she spoke these words. Their faces had turned Ice. And in all this I also met some amazing people who guided me towards the right path, who helped me find me. She looked straight towards Naina.

When she finished her address, Faith climbed down from the podium amidst some heady applaud and headed towards Naina, she felt a little uncertain on to say or how to react to her friend; that the person Naina thought she knew so well wasn't quite what she expected. But one assuring smile from Naina put her at ease. They exchanged a look that said it all…

Naina opened her arms wide to welcome her friend and Faith embraced her.

'Listen, I wanted to say something to you that I never could…that you always wanted me to', Faith whispered in Naina's ear.

'What', Naina asked.

'I love you loads Nain', Faith beamed. She had finally said it. Naina had taught her how to express her feeling openly.

'Me too silly girl !', Naina shouted aloud. 'Its time for Champagne!'

She was jubilant at her best friend's success and that Faith would now lead Stan Inc.

The strife to correct so many wrongs, the contentions that created so many rivalries, the moments of truth where everything rode in the balance, how things fell into place, how they managed the impossible and how the ultimate surreptitious plot was revealed.

They had been through so much together in the last year. Life's uncertainties and fate had brought them together and could just as easily take them away at this juncture. But, Faith and Naina would not let that happen.

"Wanna have some coffee?" asked Faith just as Naina had when they had made their first, historic trip to Barista.

❦❦❦

Faith began her story with her father's visit to her apartment just prior to her joining Stan Inc. She had not seen him in over a decade, not ever since her mother had passed away.

Her father had been driving, drunk. She had never forgiven him for the accident.

She had moved away from home on the pretense of studying abroad but when she did not return her father's calls or mail, he soon got the message that she could not live with the constant reminder that he had snatched away her family from her. He could not face her rejections and decided to let her be, hoping that someday she would bear to let him into her life again.

"I got a great education from the top institutions and was doing very well for myself. But, I realized that he was keeping close tabs on me when, after years, I received another call from him after I filed for a divorce from Rohan. Needless to say, that was probably the worst time for him to contact me." continued Faith

"So, when I opened the front door to my apartment one fine day, I was surprised. Seeing him brought back memories and, to my surprise, the good ones that I had suppressed for so long. I had lived a lonely life and so had he. He had come to me with a proposal I could not refuse."

Faith's father had built a successful BPO organization with a strong vision and values. However, he worried that he had no one to take on the legacy. He wanted his daughter to claim what was hers.

Faith did not want to be a part of his company, at first. She was independent and free and wanted to live her life that way. So, he posed Faith a business challenge. He dared her to come and work at a managerial position in one of his company's most political businesses and survive for 6 months.

Faith wondered if it would be the best career move. After all, she was holding a leadership position in one of the city's most prestigious financial institutions. She had to hide this experience in order to get her role as a Manager with CMort; else they would have deemed her as over-qualified. But, she was immensely curious about the twist to this dare and had to give it a go. Looking back now, she realized that at a subconscious level she wanted to give her father and her another try at a family. Her lonely life had matured her to appreciate that it wasn't her father who had ruined their family but her. She had not wanted to face that the accident was indeed an act of fate and had wanted so desperately to lay the blame on somebody, anybody. Seeing him after so many years, looking vulnerable yet as enigmatic as before, was critical in her accepting this feat.

During her stint with CMort, she identified with her father's words. She became his liaison and grew passionately in love with the company. She saw the beauty of the business that her dad had so fervently created and how recklessly a few folks were ruining the legacy. She had to learn more and learn from the grass roots up. She wanted to feel what the leadership rarely touch and then use that knowledge to re-create the company's culture.

She saw the pain that she had caused her dad in the past and that what had made matters worse, over the years, was her own anger and pain. She grew closer to her dad than ever before and he readied her to assume what she was born to do: Lead.

Naina smiled and Faith returned it, with renewed conviction that their friendship would survive this mission.

"So, when CMort was under threat of being pulled back, I felt like I had failed my dad. I had no control over the situation and that hurt. Edwin, being solely behind this, clearly pissed me off. But then after that call where you had to physically drag me off the phone, Edwin called me over and over again till I finally gave in. He talked, I listened. I was too tired, emotionally, to do anything else. What he told me made sense, from his perspective.

He had, over the years, seen his best friends lose jobs because so much of it was being siphoned off to India. He never understood corporate profits over long-term employee commitment. People who lost jobs had been with CMort for over 15-20 years even. He knew that, at least for the really critical work, they would have been more suited to continue to perform that job. And so, he began collecting information that would forward his case for the sake of the business as a whole. And, Surinder was running a shoddy show. So, when he dug out a ton of dirt on our processes, he also felt morally obligated to share with Pam and the rest is history."

Naina was extremely intrigued to know how then did the turnaround happen for Edwin to finally convince Pam to go ahead with BAU (business as usual)?

"Well… once Surinder was out of the scene, Edwin felt comforted. In fact, I had told my dad that Surinder was one of the major contributors in letting things get so out of hand. He has been told to put in his papers and his moving to a relationship-managing role was just for easy transitioning for all the other folks in the business. I also opened up to Edwin about my future role with the company and he felt comforted that all the skullduggery would now come to an end as I had come to find exactly what needed to be checked!"

"And Nain, let's not forget all the hard work we all put into resurrecting these processes. From introducing the knowledge management and MIS tool to doing refreshers, process automations to reducing the complexity of the forms, and all the other good stuff, was what really worked in our favor."

"Both your project as well as mine has made history at CMort, US. They are already in the process of incorporating our project learnings into their business. But, it's sad that it's I who has to tell you this instead of the rightful leadership. Dheer has only been a figurehead through this entire re-engineering process. And this company needs leaders, somebody who is operationally strong and motivated by passion for its people. Nain, I know that you have resigned but will you now come back and work alongside me? With your operational knowledge and my strategic approach, we can turn this company around." Faith urged Naina.

Naina had, however, concretized other plans for her future. She needed to focus on resurrecting her life, her creative talents and her marriage: things that made her the happiest. She had plans of exhibiting her work and perhaps travel more with Yash to his concerts.

"I can now leave peacefully Faith. I know my company and my people are in good hands', she told Faith.

Faith was disappointed yet knew that it was the right decision for Naina. She was losing a terrific worker but she had found Naina's love and had her friendship with her forever. She respected the decision Naina had made and promised her that she would leave no stone unturned to ensure that justice is served to those that deserve it.

And obviously, she had an open offer for Naina.

'If you ever think…even once, of coming back into the corporate world, I have to be the first one to know', Faith warned her mockingly. 'I cannot let anyone else take you away.'

'Promise', Naina crossed her heart.

She was sad to go. This had been her life for so long now. In one moment, her life would change.

But she knew she had to do it. She had struggled for too long, had worked too hard and had seen a lot of pain. She was tired of fighting and wanted a break. Now she wanted to rest.

With this, they raised a toast with their Barrista and Masala tea.

"To those who *Mis-guided* us to each other and our lives' true path! May we, in future, *Guide* others to theirs!"

EPILOGUE

Faith Jones was a catch and very attached. She looked stunning in a pink and green *lehenga choli*. As Naina was about to lower the *chunni* to Faith's pretty head, she caught both their reflections in the mirror of Faith's dressing table. What she saw were the faces of two ecstatic women. They had known each other for the last two years but it seemed an eternity for all that they had experienced together.

"Hey babe, come on, already. I'm getting old sittin' here." Faith egged Naina, smiling naughtily.

"What's the hurry, yaar? It's not as if Edwin has too many places he can run to!"

"Oh! Don't underestimate his resourcefulness." They laughed at their silly banter as they both remembered the events of the last year.

'*Hai*, this *lehenga* is so heavy. I can't lift it', Faith pretended to moan.

'Come on,my Angel ! If you can't lift your wedding *lehenga*, how the hell would you lift my baby !', Naina was beaming.

'Whhhat ???? Oh My God ! this is Terrific News !'

Faith jumped to hug Naina.

Time stood still as they embraced.

It seemed like eternity when they parted and looked at each other. Both were crying.

'You made my day Nain. Heartiest Congratulations to you and Yash !'

'Thanks Sweetheart. Now YOU make my day. Lets go and get you married to your *Firang*…'

They both walked hand in hand to the *mandap*.

'Where's the proud Papa by the way', Faith asked.

'He was trying to tie Edwin's *dhoti* when I saw him last', Naina laughed aloud and Faith joined in the laughter.

Here were two friends whose friendship had crossed all boundaries to develop into a relationship that was beyond this lifetime.

Their friendship had flourished even though Naina had moved on to pursue her life as an artist. Naina owned an art gallery and exhibition house and had displayed her own works on several occasions. She had gained acclaim. Spending more time with Yash had helped. They had resorted to counseling when things came to their head. It had worked

Yash and Naina were one of those lucky couples that were able to rejuvenate their relationship, as their love for each other had not diminished. It had only increased with time and their little one had brought a new zeal into their lives ! '*Ansh*' was blessed and so were they, to have him.

Over the past few years, she had found peace in a renewed relationship with her father and love with Edwin. The skeletons had steadily disintegrated as she broke through past barriers. Friendship, Family and Love, the three banes of survival for Faith stood their ground firmly and she had vowed that she would never let go.

Stan Inc. had grown, with a strong culture of boundary less ness and fair play. Professionalism was encouraged and work ethics steadily became apolitical, with her history that Faith often shared with employees as an example.

The BPO industry, like any other, has its ill wills. But, the good far outweighs the bad. It gives immense power to people to display their passion and healthy aggression to reach pinnacles to their heart's desire.

We all have a choice. A choice to make this beautiful place a better place to live in.

Naina and Faith still meet up regularly with their daughters for book shopping at OM bookstore and chit-chat over coffee at Starbucks.

You may bump into them there, someday.

NAMES
(IN ORDER OF APPEARANCE)

Faith Jones

Naina Chopra

Joe, Naina's studio assistant

Yash, Naina's husband

Randy, Naina's dog

Rohan, Faith's ex-husband

Naina's previous process: **'NIGO' (Not In Good Order) process** for **CMort**, a Mortgage Client in the BPO (Business Process Outsourcing) division in **Stan Inc**

Surinder Kumar, Naina and Faith's offensive boss

Manoj, Faith's predecessor and black belt

Anita, Assistant Manager at CMort, Surinder's pet

Paul, AVP-Quality and MBB: Faith's direct boss.

Atul, one of the managers from the 'Retirals Team', which is another big Insurance account at Stan. Naina and Atul had met during a 'Best Practice' Session couple of years back.

Fuzzy, Faith's pet dog

Mr. Chanchal "Big Shit", as people *fondly* call him heads the Financial Services vertical for Stan Inc

Manohardas Chopra: Yash's dad

Kevin: The Lead singer at the Fox

The Park: Faith's residential complex

Edwin Steel: Operations Head for CMORT, US.

Aman: Manager from the Vintage group
Pamela Watson/Pam: Edwin's big boss
Preeti: the training manager
Dheer Choudherie: the politically powerful and morally corrupt AVP, the latest entrant for CMort.
Devyani: A team member who is close to Faith and helping out with her project. She reveals the "apartment" controversy to Faith.
Vicki Manchanda: One of the Vintage Group managers handling "Vendors", a data entry process in CMort
Shantanu: A new Black belt taken on as additional support for the CMort processes.
Ranit: Naina's friend, IT Manager for CMort
Shivraj Thukral: Faith's father and CEO of Stan Inc.